FROM THE

## Secret Place

IN MY HEART

D1025228

# Christy Miller's Diary

FROM THE
## Secret Place
IN MY HEART

# ROBIN JONES GUNN

## BETHANY HOUSE PUBLISHERS
MINNEAPOLIS, MINNESOTA 55438

# My List of Friends

## Alissa
All I saw was her perfection and her gorgeous, long blond hair. I never guessed her heart carried so much pain.

## Brittany
I think Brittany and I might become good friends, even though her dad introduced me to her as "Crissy" (ugh!). She and I are both going to be sophomores, and I'm glad to know at least one person before I start this new school tomorrow.

## Doug
Hugs, hugs, hugs—Doug gives great hugs! He's a great listener, too. Tall, sandy blond hair, little-boy grin . . . that's Doug!

## Heather
Always full of advice for me about guys, Heather doesn't ever seem to have a boyfriend, I've noticed. Hmm.

## Katie

Everyone on the planet should have a true friend like Katie. Red hair is optional, but her hilarious personality is what keeps me going. Go Kelley High Cougars!

## Janelle

She has that "just flew in from Tahiti look," and she's very popular. I'll never forget the sleepover at her home, when we went out T.P.ing the most popular guy's house!

## Michael

Oh, you intriguing Irishman, you! You captured Katie's heart, and I don't know if she'll ever be the same. Of all the schools in the U.S., why did you have to come to ours?

## Paula

We've been friends since we were kids growing up in Wisconsin. But now that I'm living in California, I don't know if things can be the same between us ever again. I'm trying.

## Renee

Why do some people have to be so mean?

## Rick

Okay, so he can melt me with a single look. So what? Rick tends to have that effect on every girl I know. But he's my friend, too. At least I think he is.

## Teri

I think I'll always admire Teri for the way she stands her ground and speaks her mind. She's going to make a great cheerleader.

## Todd

From that first day on the beach, when I looked into Todd's screaming silver-blue eyes, I knew my heart would be his forever. We've been through so much over the years. The one thing that has stayed true is Todd's promise to always be my friend.

## Tracy

Tracy is so cute and petite. She's a good example to me of a gentle spirit.

# September 2

My uncle Bob gave me this diary today. He told me to try to write in it every day what I'm feeling and thinking. He said this little book might become a real friend to me.

He must have known I could really use a friend right now. This move to California and starting my sophomore year at a new school and everything is pretty scary.

So, dear diary, dear new friend, hello. What should I call you? You can call me Christy. Or Chris. Well, only a few people call me Chris. I like Christy better. Or you can call me by my full name, Christina Juliet Miller.

*Christy Miller*

*Chris Miller*

*Christina Juliet Miller*

*Christina Juliet Miller*

Actually, you aren't going to call me anything, are you? You're my silent friend. My Dear, Silent Friend. DSF. That's what I'll call you.

This is the beginning of what I hope will be a long and happy friendship, DSF.

# September 3

Well, DSF,

I should tell you about Alissa. I met her earlier this summer when I was visiting my aunt and uncle here in California. I thought I wanted to be just like Alissa, but then I found out she had a lot of difficult stuff in her life. She actually told me she thought I had it pretty good because I had a "normal" family and was still innocent.

I received a letter from her yesterday. Alissa said she didn't understand what I meant when I wrote and told her I'd given my heart to Jesus. She asked, why would I give my heart to someone who is dead, and why would I make promises to a man who no longer exists. I know she wrote that because she was thinking of her boyfriend, Shawn. When Shawn died a few months ago, she acted as if it didn't matter to her. But I know it did. It had to.

I don't know how to tell her what I believe and why I gave my heart to Christ. Maybe I can try to explain it to you, and if it sounds right, I'll write the same thing to her.

The only way I can explain my decision is that it's as if I have this secret place in my heart. Before I became a Christian, I'd go there and it always felt lonely. It was quiet. Too quiet. I could go there and be alone to think, but it was always so empty. When I surrendered my life to the Lord, it was as if He came into that secret place, and now He's there. I know He's there. He listens. He knows. He understands.

How do I explain that to someone else? Especially to Alissa, who has so much hurt in her heart. I imagine her secret place must be all closed up and locked tight. I wonder if she even goes there anymore?

## September 4
DSF, hi,

Me again. Well, I have big news. We went to Escondido today and looked at the house we're going to move into, and I think I've found my first friend. Her name is Brittany. She reminds me of Alissa in some ways. Intriguing and intimidating at the same time. She's the kind of girl I always think I want to be like, but when I'm around her I feel as though I'm not on the same level. Brittany seems so mature and experienced. Not clumsy, the way I am.

*"BFF"*

*"BFF"*

Best
Friends
Forever?

Still, I don't know. I liked having Paula as my best friend because we seemed to be the same in so many ways. At least we used to be. Now I think I'd like to be more sophisticated, like Brittany.

BFF

Things are different now that I'm here. Paula and I were close friends ever since we were little. But this summer Paula found a new best friend, and I think that, even if my family hadn't moved to California, Paula and I wouldn't be the closest of friends back at Brightwater High School.

## September 12

So much has been happening, DSF!

I haven't been able to write everything down because I don't seem to have enough time. I've been thinking about Rick, this guy I met in the craziest way. I went to a sleepover at Janelle's, and we went out to T.P. Rick's house. While we were putting the toilet paper all over Rick's place, he came out. I was hiding in the bushes, and I started to run, and . . . Oh, I don't even want to talk about it. It was the most embarrassing moment of my life.

The thing is, now Brittany says Rick has been asking about me at school. He's real tall and good-looking.

Everybody knows him. He's on the football team. I can't imagine a guy like Rick being interested in me.

What do you think?

*Rick!*

*Rick -N- Christy?*

## September 14

Dear Silent Friend of mine,

I haven't told you about Todd yet, have I? I thought of that a couple of days ago after I told you about Rick. Todd is my idea of the perfect guy. I met him this summer on the beach the same day I met Alissa and some other people. I think if I'd had you to confide in during the summer, I would have filled all your pages just talking about Todd, my summer surfer dream boy. He's not like any other guy I've ever known. You should see his screaming silver-blue eyes! And his smile . . . Oh!

*TODD -N- CHRISTY!*

Can you keep a secret? Yes, I guess you can. Todd kissed me on July 28 and gave me a bouquet of white carnations. It was the most romantic moment of my life. I still have the carnations. They're all dried out. I stuck them in a coffee can when we moved here.

However, there's one slightly huge problem with Todd. He's in Florida now at his mom's. He said he'd write me, but he never did. I think the rest of my life I'll always have sweet memories of Todd, even if we never see each other again.

## September 20

Hi, DSF,

I've been thinking about Alissa's questions from her letter some more. She asked why I'd make promises to someone who is dead, but I know now I can tell her Jesus isn't dead. He rose from the dead, and He's alive. That's what makes Christianity different from all other religions.

That's what makes it real.

I found a verse last night when I was looking in the back of my Bible for verses about the heart. It's long, but here's the whole verse, or actually three verses:

"'For I know the plans I have for you,' declares the Lord, 'plans to prosper you and not to harm you, plans to give you hope and a future. Then you will call upon me and come and pray to me, and I will listen to you. You will seek me and find me when you seek me with all your heart'" (Jeremiah 29:11–13).

I like that so much because Alissa asked why I'd make promises to a man who no longer exists. The thing is, He does exist! I made only one promise to Him—to turn over my whole life and my whole heart to Him alone. And He made all these promises to me:

—to prosper me and not to harm me

—to give me hope and a future

—to listen to me

—that I'd find Him when I seek Him with all my heart.

Okay, now I have to go write this to Alissa before I forget it all. Bye!

# September 28

I just read that last entry, DSF,

I feel bad because I never did get around to writing to Alissa. But I've been learning some new things.

Here are a few key words for you to hold on to for me. Katie Christian and Peter Pagan. At Sunday school a few days ago they talked about "missionary dating"— when you try to bring the other person up to where you are with the Lord. It's always easier for them to bring you down. I don't think I'll need to remember that for my own life, but I want to remember the thought.

My dad got really mad because I didn't tell my parents I was going out to pizza with Katie and Rick after church. Dad told me I was using up my youth too fast, and once it was gone, I wouldn't be able to get it back.

The thing is, I'm not really trying to grow up too fast. All these things are happening to me, and I'm just trying to keep up with them. I think it would be different if I were rebelling or something. But I'm trying to do the right thing.

Well, at least most of the time.

I'm sure Dad's right, that I don't always think things through. But he doesn't know all the good choices I've made or all the stuff I've already said no to.

I've been trying to figure out what God wants me to do. I think He wants me to try really hard to do the right thing and say no to everything that looks like it wouldn't be good for me.

No, no, no, no. There, my daily practice in saying no.

no!  NO?

no!

NO NO NO NO NO NO!

## October 5

Two days, DSF!

Two days until I go to Palm Springs with Janelle and Brittany! Yippee! My uncle Bob is going to a golf tournament in Palm Springs, and so my aunt invited me to come with her and to bring some friends. I wanted Katie to go with me because she's my new friend from school. I met her at Janelle's party. Katie has the prettiest red hair. It's very distinctive, and so is she. Katie is our school mascot—the Kelley High Cougar. So she can't go because of the football game on Friday night.

Janelle and Brittany are coming with me instead. I know I'm going to have a great time with both of them. They are really popular, and I think we're getting to be pretty good friends.

My little brother fell off his bike yesterday. We had to rush him to the emergency room because he was bleeding so badly, and it wouldn't stop. He ended up with four stitches, but you'd have thought it was forty the way he howled when the doctor worked on him.

Dad told me I need to help out more around the house because Mom's going to be working now. Then David begged me to wait on him because he said his chin hurt too much for him to get off the couch to get something to drink. Oh brother!

Only two more days of being everyone's slave, and then I'm off to Palm Springs. I can't wait! We are going to have so much fun!

# October 10

Oh man, oh man, my DSF!

What a nightmare I've just gone through. The trip to Palm Springs with Aunt Marti and my friends turned into a disaster. Brittany has so many problems. She lied to me a bunch of times and tried to bring me down with her. I can't believe I didn't see it coming. Am I too trusting of people or what?

I still can't believe what happened. Brittany got Janelle and me in trouble with the police when she shop-lifted and stole prescription diet pills. Then she and Janelle ran from the security guard and left me alone! I can't believe I'm even writing this down. It was the worst thing I've ever gone through in my life. We had to come home from Palm Springs early, and everything was ruined.

Tracy sent me a note before we went to Palm Springs. She wrote out a verse that really helped me when we went through that whole thing with the police and the questioning. I promised myself I'd look up the verse in my Bible and underline it. I also want to write it here so you can remind me, DSF, how much that verse meant to me when I need-ed it most. Here it is:

"The LORD himself goes before you and will be with

you; he will never leave you nor forsake you. Do not be afraid; do not be discouraged" (Deuteronomy 31:8).

My dad put me on restriction. Two weeks of no social activities. The only thing that's going to be hard is not going to church and seeing Rick. I never see him at school.

The other afternoon at Pizza Hut was the best time I've had since we moved here. Rick's probably already forgotten about it. He'll probably have another girlfriend by the time I get off restriction.

Why do guys do that? They act interested in you, and then they forget about you.

Like Todd. I'll never forget Todd. Ever. But I bet if he saw me right now, he wouldn't even remember my name. If only guys weren't so weird. If only they

## October 11

Sorry I stopped in the middle of a sentence yesterday, DSF.

I was dropping off into the land of "If Only," and with all that had gone wrong in my life, I knew I'd end up getting depressed and staying very depressed thinking about Todd and Rick.

Then guess what happened today? Rick asked me to homecoming. No, of course I'm not going. My parents are really strict about dating. But you know what he said? He said the most beautiful girls are the innocent ones. And that my honesty intrigued him. He also said that, for a girl like me, he could wait until I was old enough to be allowed to go out with him. That means my sixteenth birthday next July 27. He was so sweet and understanding. He said he'd see me at church on Sunday and that he'd call me sometime. I'm so glad I'm not on phone restriction along with everything else!

And *then,* as if that wasn't enough to make my day, I came home and the phone rang. David said it was a guy, and so, of course, I thought it was Rick. I picked up the phone and said, "Hi, Rick," but it wasn't Rick!

It was *Todd*!

He was calling me from his mom's in Florida. I had almost given up on ever hearing from him since it's been almost three months. His voice sounded sooooo good! We talked a really long time. I told him all about Palm Springs, and he told me this long story about letting go of things that I didn't need to hold on to anymore. That was what I've been trying to do by learning to say no. But then Todd said it wasn't enough just to say no. I needed to start saying yes to the right stuff. I especially need to start saying yes to God. It was so cool.

And the best news of all is that Todd is moving back to California. He's going to be here by Christmas. I can't wait to see him again!

This has been such a perfect day! After everything turned into such a disaster last weekend, it's as if God is turning everything around for good.

I'm so happy right now. I really, honestly feel peace in that secret place in my heart. I haven't felt this close to God since last summer on the beach with Todd, Doug, and Tracy and all the other Christians I met. I wish we could all get together, sit around the campfire pit on the beach, and sing again.

Todd said when he comes at Christmas he wants us to have breakfast on the beach. That is going to be so awesome (to use Doug's word)! Todd told me to start practicing making scrambled eggs.

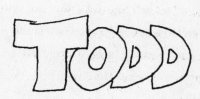

Well, I better go. I finally did write Alissa, and I told her Jesus wasn't dead. He's very much alive and very present in my life. I forgot to tell her all the other stuff from that verse about the plans God has for us. Maybe God had me find that verse just for me because it really is true in my life right now. I know God has a plan to give me hope and a future. All I pray is that I will keep seeking Him with my whole heart.

You keep reminding me of that, okay, DSF? I'm counting on you to hold these words for me so I can come back and read them again when I need to be reminded. Okay? Thank you, my Dear Silent Friend. What would I do without you? DSF

## November 27

Dear Friend who happens to be silent,

I wish you could speak up now. I need some advice. I'm starting to buy Christmas presents, and I don't know what to do. Should I buy something for Todd? I'm pretty sure I'm going to get something for Rick. But what should I buy them? Is it strange to give gifts to two different guys? Well? Speak up!

## December 21

Dear Silent Friend,

KISSES

Todd /
Rick //

Now I'm glad you can't speak. I need you to hold another secret for me. I saw Rick tonight, and do you know what happened? He kissed me. It was quick and sort of pushy, if you know what I mean. I didn't expect it at all.

Then I gave him the CD I bought him, and he kissed me again. The second kiss was longer, and I knew he was going to do it. And you know what I did? I pulled away. Then it got all awkward, and he said we should go back in the church gym. But it was like he was mad at me.

The worst part was that afterward he totally ignored me. I don't know what I should have done differently. I feel so mixed up right now.

I've thought about kisses before, you know. I think that's normal—to wonder what it would be like to be kissed. But I never thought seriously about kissing Rick. I guess I wasn't ready. Maybe I should think this through some more before I see him again. That is, if he's still speaking to me.

## December 22

Okay, DSF,

Now all I can think about are kisses and kissing. I'm going to see Todd in a few days. What if he kisses me again like he did last summer? How many kisses do I want to give away? I've never thought this through before. I think kisses should mean something very special and should be given away very sparingly while I'm young.

I'm fifteen, you know. Does that seem young to you? It does to me. At least it does today.


## December 25

**Christmas Day**

Well, DSF,

After all these long weeks of waiting, I finally saw Todd this morning. We had breakfast on the beach, as he promised. And now I'm perplexed.

It seems that when dreams come true, they never turn out the same way you dreamed them. They twist and turn and disappoint, leaving you wanting so much more. I don't know which to blame: the dream itself or the reality that dissolves the dream.

Todd Spencer

Surely Todd Spencer is the most noncommittal guy on the face of the Earth. He spent more time skim boarding on the beach with David this morning than with me. And then he took off right after we were done eating, or should I say, done eating what the sea gulls left for us. He said he was going to Shawn's parents' house because this is the first Christmas since Shawn died. I know that was a good thing for Todd to do and a good reason for him to leave, but I can barely describe to you how I felt as I sat alone by the dwindling fire, watching him walk away. He was supposed to have his arms around me. Instead, his arms were full of camping gear.

He didn't even look back.

That was our dream breakfast, and it was over almost before it began. I'd have to say the best word to describe what I felt was "abandoned." I felt forsaken. I know God will never abandon me or forsake me. I guess friends do sometimes. Even special friends. Even Todd.

All I can say is that this week I have to find out where I stand with Todd. I need to know where our relationship is and where it's going. This is too important to me just to let it slip away.

## December 27

You aren't going to be very proud of me, my Dear Silent Friend.

I played some pointless games today with my friends. The thing is, at the time, it didn't seem like they were games or that I was doing anything I'd regret later. But now I feel awful. I wish I had this day to live over again.

You see, we all went ice-skating. Heather told me I should try to make Todd jealous by skating with Doug. Then Doug asked me to skate, and we were pretty good. And it was fun. But you should have seen the way Todd looked at us.

Then we went to eat, and Todd kept giving me these puppy-dog looks, as if he wanted me to sit next to him. Or maybe he just wanted me to see how left out he felt. I know I've felt that way lots of times. Like last summer when Todd took me to a concert. I thought just the two of us were going, but then it ended up being a whole bunch of people who were already friends, and I felt so left out.

It didn't get much better today after we left the restaurant. Doug gave me his jacket before we went into the restaurant because I was so cold. Then Tracy was saying how cold she was when we left so I gave his jacket to her. She gave me the strangest look. Then I figured it out. She didn't want Doug's jacket. She wanted Doug to put his arm around her! Tracy likes Doug!

Tracy ♡'s Doug

I didn't see it before, but it makes sense now. When she and I were making cookies the other day, she said she was going to give some to a guy she liked, but she wouldn't tell me who he was. Now I know. It was Doug! I spent the whole day skating and everything with Doug, and she must have been so jealous.

I have a headache thinking about all this. How am I going to patch things up so we can all be friends again?

I'm only staying here at the beach with my aunt and uncle for the rest of this week, and then I go back home to Escondido. I'm not looking forward to going to school after Christmas vacation and running into Rick.

Why does life have to be so complicated?

## December 28

I'm back, DSF,

As if that last entry wasn't enough to keep me tossing and turning all night, guess who sent me a letter here at my aunt and uncle's house?

Alissa.

She said she had lost my address in Escondido. And that's not all she said. She told me she's pregnant. My hand is shaking as I write this. She's pregnant. I still can't believe it. I started to cry so hard when I read her letter. She asked me to pray for her, and I did. A lot. I fell asleep for a while, and now it's the middle of the night and very quiet. I think I woke up because I have so much on my mind. My body fell asleep, but my mind didn't. It kept going and going until all my wild dreams woke me up.

The only good thing about all this is that Alissa said she had thought about having an abortion but then had changed her mind because a friend of hers had one a few years ago but then wished she hadn't. Alissa said she'd probably have the baby and give it up for adoption. I pray that's what she does. Alissa also said she went to a Crisis Pregnancy Center, and the counselor there gave her a Bible.

I pray Alissa reads that Bible until the words break through into that secret place in her heart. God's words are like rays of light. They can slip through the tiniest opening and make all the darkness instantly disappear.

I know that's true for Alissa, but it's also true for me and my problems with my friends—although my problems seem like nothing compared to what Alissa is going through. Her dad is dead, and her mom is an alcoholic. Alissa doesn't have any brothers or sisters. What would I be like if I were in her situation, or if I'd been through all the things she's been through?

Oh, dear Father God, please be extra close to Alissa right now. Shine your light into the hurt and darkness in her life so she can see you and call out to you and trust in you. Please break through the powers of darkness that have a chain around her heart. Break through and shine your light there. I want her to come to know you. Amen.

## December 29

DSF,

Today was one of those battles with my controlling aunt. She took me shopping and wanted me to get my hair cut again. I didn't do it. But I also didn't keep a bad attitude about it all day. Well, except for when Aunt Marti and I got into an argument at the restaurant because she said she thought Alissa was so perfect and I should try to be more like her. I blurted out that Alissa was pregnant and asked my aunt if that's what she wanted for me, too. She got soooo mad! But that's another story.

What I wanted to write down were the words to this praise song I kept singing over and over in my head, like a prayer, when we were at the hair salon.

Touch this heart, so full of pain,
Heal it with your love.
Make it soft and warm again,
Melt me with your love.
I don't want to push you away,
Come back in
Come to stay.
Make me tender, just like you.
Melt me with your love.

I wish I could be soft and tender all the time. Oh, and I should tell you what happened after we got back from shopping. Doug was here. He said my hair smelled like green apples. Then, while we were in front of my aunt and uncle's house, he leaned over to smell my hair. At that exact moment, Todd went driving by in his old VW bus! I'm pretty sure he saw us. I wish Todd would have stopped. Then he would have seen nothing is going on between Doug and me. Really. I'm sure it didn't look that way just driving by.

If Todd had stopped, then he would have heard Doug tell me he was going to take Tracy out. I was really happy about that because she likes him. If Todd finds out Doug is dating Tracy, then Todd won't think I was trying to get Doug interested in me while we were ice-skating.

## January 1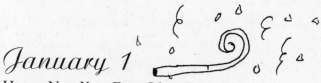

Happy New Year, Dear Silent Friend!

What a New Year's Eve I had last night! Where do I begin? First, my aunt surprised me by inviting Todd to come to her house for a fancy New Year's Eve dinner. I didn't know he was there, so when I walked downstairs and heard someone playing the mandolin in the living room, I thought my aunt had hired someone to play music while we ate. I know that sounds crazy, but if you knew my aunt, that's exactly the kind of thing she would do.

When I saw that it was Todd, I almost screamed! He'd told me earlier he had plans for the evening, and I thought he was going out with another girl. I never guessed the plans were with me!

After the fancy dinner, we went to Heather's house

for a party, and on the way I told Todd about Alissa and the baby. He's sure that the baby is Shawn's, which shocked me. I hadn't tried to figure out who the father was.

Then Todd said the most amazing thing. He said that even though what Shawn and Alissa did was wrong, they created a human life and that life had something that was going to last forever—a soul. Then he said, "Even angels can't do that."

That really stunned me when I thought about it later. I will never think of people the same way again. Every human has a soul. And every soul will last forever. Where that soul spends eternity depends on how that person chooses to respond to God. I'm still amazed by that thought.

But anyway, there's something else to tell you. When Todd and I left the party, we were driving back to my aunt and uncle's in Gus. (I told you about Gus, didn't I? Gus the bus? Todd's old VW van?) We finally got to talk about "us," and we both said we wanted to be the kind of friends who were friends forever.

Then Todd stopped at this intersection. He pulled me out of the van, and when we stood in front of the head-lights, I realized it was "our" intersection—the place where we stood last summer when he kissed me good-bye before I left to go back home to Wisconsin.

I was laughing and telling him this was crazy, and then he gave me this bracelet. It's so beautiful. I love it! It's a gold ID bracelet with the word "Forever" engraved on it. That's when he told me that no matter what happened in the future, we would be friends forever.

I'm smiling so big right now. I've never felt like this before in my whole life. And I think part of the reason is because this bracelet represents more than just Todd or my forever friendship with him. Every time I look at this bracelet, it will remind me of the eternal part of me that's going to go on forever. My heart and soul belong to God, and I am His forever!

KISSES

RICK ||
TODD ||

# January 14

Dear SF,

Do you know what today is? It's Todd's birthday. I know. I didn't know it, either. I can't believe I never asked him when his birthday was. I feel really bad because I didn't get him a card or anything. I found out it was his birthday because Doug called and said they were going to have a party for him over at Tracy's, and Doug asked if I could go up to Newport Beach for the party. It's an hour and a half drive to my aunt and uncle's house.

I was so upset because I couldn't work out any way to get there, and my aunt and uncle are going away this weekend so I'd have to stay at Tracy's. My mom didn't think that was a good idea. So I'm not going.

My parents let me call Todd and talk to him for a long time after school today. I spent the first ten minutes apologizing. Todd, in his usual, ultracasual way, kept telling me not to worry about it. I told him I hoped we could see each other again soon, and he said he might be able to come down here next weekend. I sure hope it works out!

If he comes, maybe I can bake a belated birthday cake for him or give him a present then. But what? Guys are so hard to buy for. Remember when I didn't know what to get Rick or Todd?

Well, Rick has done a good job of avoiding me lately. I think he's going out with one of the cheerleaders.

# February 19

Dear Silent Friend,

You know how some people have a bad Valentine's Day? Well, I've had a bad Valentine's week! Katie talked me into making a valentine for Todd. Have I told you about Katie? She's my closest friend now, and she's a lot of fun. She usually has great ideas. Except for this valentine idea.

Should I tell you? Okay, but don't mock me. I've had enough humiliation for one week. I wanted to buy something nice for Todd to make up for not getting him anything for his birthday. Katie convinced me to write Todd a little message from those sugar candy hearts that have the words on them. I glued candy hearts all over the top of this little box. The messages on the hearts formed a sentence. It said, "Be True, My Pal, Call Me, Can't Wait, Your Gal."

I know. It sounds really silly, but they don't give you a whole lot to work with on those hearts. Just a few words.

Then, inside the little box, I put a phone card with thirty minutes of credit on it. I wrapped it up in red and white tissue paper with hearts on it, put the package in a padded mailer, and sent it off to Todd a week before Valentine's Day.

So do you think "My Pal" called me? No. I waited all Valentine's Day. No call. I didn't expect him to send me a card. He never writes me. But with the calling card, I figured he'd have everything he needed to call and wish me a happy Valentine's Day. I waited five days for him to call and got more and more depressed each day.

Today I was over at Katie's, and she convinced me to call him. She said it didn't matter that it was long distance as long as I only talked to him about five minutes. I figured five minutes was all I needed to check in to make sure he was okay. I haven't heard from him in two weeks, but with Todd, I'd never know if he was just busy or if he was unconscious in some hospital.

I called, and he answered on the second ring. He acted like nothing was wrong. He talked about how the waves were up for the winter swell and how he went surfing this morning. After about four minutes, I finally asked if he received my Valentine's present. He said, "Yeah, but why didn't you put the candy hearts inside the box? I had to peel off the glue before I ate them."

I practically screamed in the phone at him. You should have seen my face! Katie was fanning me, as if she thought I was going to pass out. I must have gotten pretty red. Then I asked if he liked the phone card and he said, "Oh yeah. Thanks. It came in handy the other day when Gus broke down and I didn't have any money on me to call a tow truck. If I hadn't put your phone card in my wallet, I'd probably still be stuck down in San Clemente."

Can you see why I said it was a disaster of a Valentine's Day? No cards. No call. Todd *ate* my secret message and used *our* thirty minutes of phone time to chat with some tow truck driver!

Now Katie is telling me I need to think of a better idea for an Easter present for Todd, but I'm telling her I'm not in the mood to lay any more eggs, decorated or not!

# March 28

Don't have much time, DSF,

But wanted to write down the words to a song I heard today before I forget it. I don't remember all the words, but here's part of the song:

> You never gave up on me,
> Your arms are still open

Waiting for me
So here I come.
I got your invitation,
Here I come.
No more hesitation,
Here I come
Back to your heart again.

It has a really pretty tune. It made me think of God and how He's always waiting for me with open arms. He's my Valentine every day of the year.

By the way, it's a week until Easter, and I decided not to send anything to Todd. He's been calling me a little more often, and I think he might come down here to Escondido to see me during Easter vacation. But it's an hour and a half drive each way. I don't know if old Gus is able to come this far.

I've begun to realize that this really, truly is a friendship with Todd. It's not a boyfriend-girlfriend thing, even though he gave me the bracelet and kissed me and everything.

In some ways I wish he hadn't kissed me because that makes me think it's more of a boyfriend-girlfriend relationship. But his kisses both times—when he gave me the flowers and when he gave me the bracelet—were short and sweet and not a mushy, movie kind of grab-her-and-kiss-her-good kiss. And they weren't pushy kisses like Rick's two kisses were.

I wonder what kisses mean to Todd? I think they mean something different to him than they do to Rick. Maybe I'm making more of all this than I should. Todd's and my relationship, or should I say friendship, is so eternally knit together, yet at the same time it's held really loosely. I can't figure it out.

Oh well, I've gotta fly. My dad is taking us out to dinner for my mom's birthday, and I think everyone is about ready to go.

## April 10

Dear Silent Friend,

I haven't told you yet, but I'm going to try out for cheerleading. I've been swamped with school stuff and church activities and now cheerleading practice. I talked to Todd about it, and he thinks if I do this I should do it for the Lord because, if I become a cheerleader, I'll have an audience. People will be watching me and watching how I react in certain situations. Maybe I should pray more about this.

Lord, I want to do this cheerleading thing for you. I know Todd's right—that if I become a cheerleader, people will look up to me and respect me. That will give me a better chance to tell them that I'm a Christian and maybe invite them to church or something. I just want whatever is best, and I want to be a good example to others. Amen.

I talked to Rick after school today. He was so sweet. Sometimes that guy can say just the right thing. For several months I hardly ever saw him. Now he's being super friendly again. I was getting discouraged about trying out for cheerleading, but he convinced me I should give it my best effort. He said I have "killer eyes," and that it's because of my innocence.

I told him he makes me feel like Play-Doh, and then he hugged me right when Renee, my major rival for cheerleader, walked by. At cheerleading practice she kept giving me the dirtiest looks. I know she would love it if I dropped out. But I'm not going to. Not now. I'm committed.

Katie hasn't been as supportive of all this as I thought she would be, but then all she's talked about lately is who is going to the prom with whom, so there's not much point in talking to her about anything else. I wonder if Todd is thinking about asking me to his prom. He's a senior, and all seniors go to their proms, don't they?

# April 13

My Dearest Silent Friend,

Earlier tonight I thought about writing to you about this enchanted spring evening. I really, really thought tonight was going to be a memory I'd always save in my "Todd" scrapbook. And I guess I will, but not for the reasons I thought I was going to.

When Todd came for dinner tonight, he asked if we could go for a walk. We went for ice cream, and on the way, he held my hand and recited some verses to me from 1 Corinthians 13. The verses were about love, and I thought he and I were having about the most romantic evening in the whole world.

Then we got to the ice cream parlor, and everything went crazy. Katie came in and told me she told Rick I was going to ask him to the prom. Then Rick came in, and he and Todd "met" by bumping into each other. Rick didn't realize I was with Todd, so he came over and sat by me, like he was waiting to start talking to me, as if we already had plans to go to the prom. Then Todd came back, and oh, man, what a disaster!

Why do these tragedies always find me?

Todd and I walked home, and we had this argument-ish discussion. I started to cry. I apologized later, but Todd said I didn't need to apologize. Then, just when I thought everything was clearing up and going back to being cozy between Todd and me, he told me he's going to the prom with a girl from his school named Jasmine!

I'm crying again now. Sorry if my tears are getting your pages wet.

About an hour ago everyone else went to bed. It's been painfully quiet around here. I took off my Forever bracelet and buried it along with all my romantic feelings for Todd. I put it in with the dead carnation petals from that first bouquet he gave me. You know how I told you I've been keeping them in an old Folgers coffee can? Well, now the brown carnations and the bracelet are both buried in the deepest corner of my closet.

If I could only bury my feelings as easily, I could get some sleep. I can't sleep at all. I can't stop crying, either. I sure don't feel like praying right now. Oh, DSF, do you have any idea how deep this hurt is?

# May 2

I haven't paid you a visit for quite some time, have I, DSF?

I just read that part I wrote about how I wanted to become a cheerleader for God but above all to pursue this cheerleading dream so I could be a good example of a Christian. Well, that's been a lot harder than I thought it would be. And it seems like I ended up doing it more for me than for God.

But I won! I'm on the squad. And since I'm a cheerleader, I'm going to do it for you now, Lord. I'm going to let all the girls on the squad know I'm a Christian. I'm going to be a good example of you to them and to the whole school.

*Christina Miller —*

*CHEERLEADER!*

## May 18

DSF,

Since that last entry so much has happened. I gave up my cheerleading spot for Teri, since she's going to be a senior next year and I'm only going to be a junior. Teri deserved to be on the squad. I know she would have won instead of me if she hadn't twisted her ankle at tryouts. This probably all sounds dramatic, but the decision seemed pretty obvious. I feel really good about it.

What I don't feel good about is that Todd surprised me by coming to the assembly when next year's squad was announced. He showed me pictures from his prom—that's the part that made me feel bad. It turns out Jasmine was in a car accident a while ago, and now she's permanently in a wheelchair. What actually happened was Todd took her to dinner with their friends, but they didn't go to the dance. Jasmine looked so happy in that photo. I was ashamed of myself for being so jealous and so mad at Todd.

Now I'm glad he took Jasmine. I'm glad I didn't go to the prom at my school, either. Katie went with Lance and had an okay time—until she ended up going home by herself, which was pretty low of Lance to send her off like that while he stayed.

Anyway, I think things are sort of smoothed over with

Rick after the whole prom mix-up. He's speaking to me, at least.

## June 6

Hello, DSF!

This Thursday is the last day of school, and Katie and I are going to have a party at my house with just the two of us to celebrate. It's been quite a year. I can't believe how fast it's gone. I'm more ready for summer vacation than I've ever been in my life!

## July 5

Hello, DSF,

How are you? I'm happy. I'm having a great summer so far. We celebrated the Fourth of July at my aunt and uncle's yesterday. Todd was there, and we went for a long walk on the beach at sunset. My brother and my mom came with us on the walk, but it was still fun and kind of romantic, even though we didn't hold hands or anything.

Todd is going to Hawaii in three weeks with my uncle, which I think is totally unfair. Oh, sure, he has to help paint Bob's two condos, but Todd will still have plenty of time for fun. And three long weeks of it!

Paula, my old friend from Wisconsin, is coming to stay with me for two weeks while Todd is in Hawaii, so I can't exactly complain. I'm looking forward to seeing her, but I'm pretty nervous about it, too. We haven't seen each other in a year, and if Paula has changed as much as I have, then we'll probably be like two strangers trying to become friends. Paula will be here for my sixteenth birthday on July 27th, but Todd won't be. Sigh. Seems like I never can have everything the way I want it.

P.S.—Katie took her driver's license test today, and she missed one too many on the written part so she has to go back and take it again tomorrow. Then she'll probably have to wait a week or so before she can take the driving part. I'm halfway through driver's training summer school classes, and my dad's been taking me out to practice driving. He makes me sooooo nervous! I'll be glad when driver's training is over, but then I'll really be nervous about taking my driver's test. Especially since Katie said her brothers told her the written part was easy, and then she didn't pass it.

Well, one worry at a time. And right now my next worry is getting ready to go baby-sit. I'm glad I keep getting asked to baby-sit for these three families because I really need the money. But the last time I sat for this little boy he was such a brat. He wouldn't mind me at all. I hope he's better this time!

# July 27

Hold this for me, DSF.

Dear Future Husband,

I turned sixteen today, and I know it may seem weird writing this to you now, but this letter is sort of my way of making a promise to you in writing.

Maybe I already know you, or maybe we haven't met yet. Either way, I want to save myself for you. I want my whole self, my heart and body and everything, to be a present I'll give you on our wedding day.

I don't care how long it takes or how hard it gets, but I promise you I won't let anybody else "unwrap" me so on our wedding night I'll be the kind of gift you'll be happy to receive.

I know I have a lot of years ahead of me before we get married, whoever you are. That's why I want to make this promise now so that no matter whom I go out with, I'll always think of myself as a present I want to give to you alone one day.

I also want to start to pray for you—wherever you are, whoever you are—that God will prepare you for me and that you'll save all of yourself for me, too.

I already love you.

Your future wife,

*Christina Juliet Miller*

# August 10

Aloha, DSF!

I wrote that letter to my future husband when we were in Hawaii. My aunt surprised us after we picked up Paula from the airport by saying we were all going to Maui to spend the week with Uncle Bob and Todd. It was a dream come true, but even before we left I found myself wishing Katie was coming with me instead of Paula. Katie and I have grown so close this past year, and while Paula and I tried to pick up where we left off in our friendship, we both had changed too much. Then, when we got to Maui, Paula seemed set on capturing all of Todd's attention, which made me furious.

On my birthday we went swimming in this cove where we could snorkel and see lots of fish. I loved it! Todd came swimming out to my raft, and we talked. It was like nothing had changed between us just because Paula was flirting with him.

That was my favorite part of my birthday because the morning was a disaster, and the luau and hula show with everyone that evening wasn't exactly my idea of a good time. I mean, it was a good time, but I would have been just as happy walking barefoot along the beach holding hands with Todd. At the luau, they chose certain guests to go up on the stage and dance the hula, and it was so embarrassing.

## August 11

Aloha, again, DSF!

I had to go to the grocery store with my mom, so I had to stop writing that last entry before I told you everything about Hawaii. It's almost midnight now, and everyone else is asleep. I like summer nights like this when it's warm and quiet. My window is open, and I can hear the nighttime critters out there making all their happy summer sounds. There's one cricket or frog or something that keeps singing one high note over and over. Maybe it's a bird.

I can smell the jasmine from the front of the house. It's so sweet! I'd love to stay up all night.

Now, on to the rest of the Maui trip.

The big adventure of the week was when we went to Hana and then to some waterfalls and pools where we went swimming. Todd jumped off this bridge—his bridge. When he was a kid he went camping with his dad in that part of Maui, and his dad jumped off the bridge into the pool of water below, but Todd couldn't jump because the bridge was so high. He decided he wanted to jump now, and he did.

Later, Todd called it "our" bridge. He gave me a poster of the bridge for my birthday because it was a place that had good memories for him. Now it has good memories for both of us. I have the poster up in my room right now.

I ended up having to drive over the bridge because a bee stung Todd, and his foot swelled horribly. He's allergic to beestings, and he had to give himself a shot, but it still took a long time for the swelling to go down. He couldn't drive the Jeep, and it was starting to get dark. Paula couldn't drive because she didn't have her glasses with her, so it was up to me.

And I did it. I overcame my fears of driving, and it became a forever kind of moment for Todd and me. I'm sure I'll always remember that day because so much happened.

But when I think about it now, what I remember most is the way Hana smelled after it rained. It was a warm, earthy, freshly washed kind of smell. I can't explain it, but I miss that smell. I miss the sound of the palm trees when the wind rushes through them. I miss the fragrance of the white plumeria flowers and the sound of the ocean taking deep, long sighs and then letting them out on the shore. I miss Maui. I want to go back.

# *September 19*

I have a job! What do you think of that, DSF?

My first job.

And it was such an easy interview. Can you guess where I'm working?

The pet store at the mall. It was Katie's suggestion. She said that since I used to live on a farm, I should get a job with animals. The thing I didn't tell Katie or my new boss, Jon, is that I'm not particularly crazy about animals. I mean, I like them and everything, but I never was one of those girls who had her room covered with posters of horses. And when we had pets back in Wisconsin, they were just "around." I never had one precious, favorite pet that stayed in my room or anything.

The most embarrassing part of my interview was that my dad took me, and he stayed there, acting like he was a customer or something. The only problem was he didn't act like a customer. He kept looking at me while I was filling out the papers, and he walked over closer when Jon started to ask me questions.

The worst part was that my dad was wearing his overalls from the dairy where he works. He looked really out of place at the mall. It was embarrassing being with him, but at the same time, I was really glad he was there. I love my dad the way he is. Truly. It's a strange thing. I feel embarrassed being with him at times, but I wouldn't want him to change a bit because he's my dad. It's the same way with my mom. I wonder if anyone else ever feels this way about their parents.

## September 20

DSF, I have a headache.

I think I got it from Rick. Is it possible to get a headache from a guy? I have so much to tell you about Rick. I guess I didn't want to write to you about him because I haven't figured out exactly what's going on. I thought if I tried to write about everything, I'd just fill pages and pages of craziness. So instead of long ramblings, here are a few thoughts.

1. Rick likes me. That's a nice thing. I like that he's acted interested in me for a long time.
2. I like the way Rick makes me feel. It's different from what I've felt with any other guy. I can't explain it except to say that Rick makes me want to be a better person for him.
3. Whatever is happening between Rick and me right now, I don't know what to do with it. I think I have

to let things go the way they're going to go and be wise—whatever that means.

Rick???

## September 26

Did I say "wise" last time I wrote to you, DSF?

I guess I did. I think I've been wise with Rick. The thing nobody ever tells you is that "wise" might be good and right and the best way to go, but it can also bring an immense amount of pain.

Rick is a thief. There. I said it. He stole my Forever bracelet that Todd gave me, and he traded it at a jewelry store for a clunky silver one with his name engraved on it. When I figured that out today, and he finally admitted it, I told him I couldn't go out with him anymore. It was the biggest, most agonizing scene you could imagine. I still can't believe what happened. And it hurts so much. I'd tell you all the gory details, but I'm too exhausted right now. Besides, I don't think I'll have to record this day to remember it the rest of my life. If anything, I wish I could erase this day.

Rick

# September 27

Dear SF,

I read a poem aloud in class today, and I felt as if this poet, Christina Rossetti, knew me and knew all about what has been happening in my life these past few weeks. The amazing part is that she lived more than 150 years ago in London, and yet she expressed exactly what I felt. It made me think of how it doesn't matter when or where we live because women are the same everywhere and in every generation. We share the same kinds of hopes and dreams and fears and hurts.

The poem is kind of long, but it's really good. Here's Christina's poem "Twice." (And isn't it interesting that she and I even share the same first name? I'm definitely going to look her up in heaven!)

> I took my heart in my hand
> (O my love, O my love),
> I said: Let me fall or stand,
> Let me live or die,
> But this once hear me speak—
> (O my love, O my love)—
> Yet a woman's words are weak;
> You should speak, not I.

You took my heart in your hand
With a friendly smile,
With a critical eye you scanned,
Then set it down,
And said: It is still unripe,
Better wait awhile:
Wait while the skylarks pipe,
Till the corn grows brown.

I have to stop and make a comment here, DSF. I didn't tell you about what happened with Todd. I only reported on the agonizing breakup with Rick. But I have a whole different story about Todd. Rick took me to dinner in Newport Beach, and if you can believe it, Doug was the valet who parked the car! Doug convinced Rick that we should stop by at a party at Tracy's house, and Todd was there. I'd only seen Todd twice since our big trip to Maui, and he's called a few times. I honestly thought that if Todd really cared about me, he'd say something to me at the party. But he didn't.

I stayed at my aunt and uncle's house, and the next morning I couldn't sleep so I went for a lonely walk on the beach. Todd was on the beach, too. He came and sat by me. I pulled out all the courage I had and I told Todd how I felt about him. He said I should be free to go out with whomever I wanted and that it was selfish of him to try to hold on to me while he waited for me to grow up.

It was just like this poem! I held my heart out, and Todd basically said it wasn't ripe. Here's the rest of the poem:

> As you set it down it broke—
> Broke, but I did not wince;
> I smiled at the speech you spoke,
> At your judgment that I heard:
> But I have not often smiled
> Since then, nor questioned since,
> Nor cared for corn-flowers wild,
> Nor sung with the singing bird.
>
> I take my heart in my hand,
> O my God, O my God,
> My broken heart in my hand:
> Thou hast seen, judge Thou.
> My hope was written on sand,

(Is this my life or what? "My hope was written on sand.")

> O my God, O my God;
> Now let Thy judgment stand—
> Yea, judge me now.

This contemned of a man,
This marred one heedless day,
This heart take Thou to scan
Both within and without:

Refine with fire its gold,
Purge Thou its dross away—
Yea hold it in Thy hold,
Whence none can pluck it out.

I take my heart in my hand—
I shall not die, but live—
Before Thy face I stand;
I, for Thou callest such
All that I have I bring,
All that I am I give,
Smile Thou and I shall sing
But shall not question much.

Every time I read this poem I know I'll remember that morning on the beach with Todd. I didn't tell you what happened after he said I needed to grow up. He told me he was going to Oahu. Yes, Oahu, as in Hawaii. He left the next day and is staying with his friend Kimo. Not for a visit but to live.

I know I thought I would never see Todd again when

he moved to his mom's in Florida. Now I really know he's gone for good. I wish I could tell you how I feel about that, but I'm not sure. I feel like Christina said in her poem, that I'm turning over my broken heart to God and I'll wait on Him and trust Him.

## October 22

Dearest, kindest, gentlest of all Silent Friends,

I think you'd like my English teacher. I really like the kind of assignments she's been giving us. First that poetry assignment when I discovered Christina Rossetti, and now we have to write about friends. Maybe I should write about you and the joys of trusting all my secrets to a Dear Silent Friend.

Here are some of the quotes from the paper she gave us with the assignment:

"Friendship? Yes, please!" Charles Dickens

"My treasures are my friends." Constantine

"Friendship is rarer than love and more enduring." Jeremy Taylor

"The language of friendship is not words, but meanings. It is an intelligence above language." Henry David Thoreau

"The only way to have a friend is to be one." Ralph Waldo Emerson

"Friendship is like a sheltering tree." Samuel Taylor Coleridge

"There is no friend like an old friend, who has shared our morning days, no greeting like his welcome, no homage like his praise." Oliver Wendell Holmes

I'd like to add my own thought about friendship.

"Friends come and go, but true, forever friends are never farther away than the secret corner of your heart."

*Christina Juliet Miller*

# November 1

Okay, laugh now, DSF, and avoid the rush.

I agreed to join the ski club with Katie, and now we're going on a trip over Thanksgiving to Lake Tahoe. I know, I know. Me on skis. This ought to be interesting.

We're trying to sell candy bars to raise money for our trip, but Katie keeps eating all of her candy. I took some to work, and Jon was so nice. He let me put them out at the cash register. People are actually buying them! I do have the nicest boss ever. He's a unique guy, but he's been very understanding lately.

Christy + Katie = SKI BUNNIES!

# November 9

Hello there, DSilentF!

Tonight at youth group, Luke asked us to write out what we're thankful for. Here's my list:

"I'm thankful for my parents, this house, my health, and all the blessings God has given us, like food and clothes. I'm thankful for my friends and . . . I'm thankful for Todd. And Rick. And Katie. And for my job, my church, my relationship with Jesus, and the way I can talk with Him anytime and anywhere. Amen."

That's what I wrote. I was a little surprised that both Todd and Rick made the list, since they have both vanished from my life. But then I realized that I'm thankful for what I learned from both of them. Not that it was always easy or fun. I'm not thankful for the pain. But I'm thankful for the experiences and what I gained from them.

# November 28

Well, DSF, I saw Rick.

He came by with Doug on Sunday. I was asleep on the couch because I was so tired from the ski trip, which, by the way, was an entire adventure in itself. First I'll tell you about Rick. He barely looked at me. He was getting a ride back to college with Doug, and since Doug wanted to stop by my house, Rick had to come, too.

I think Rick is one of those guys who is all or nothing. Either I'm completely devoted to him or I'm on his list of people to ignore. I wish it weren't like that. That's one of the things I like about Todd. He's the same with everybody all the time. Todd takes his friendships seriously.

Although, what am I saying? Todd, the great silent one, the one who is even more silent than you right now, is still in Hawaii. I guess. Doug didn't say anything about Todd, so I guess he is still over there surfing his little heart out.

Rick noticed that I had Todd's bracelet back on my wrist. I could tell he was pretty surprised about that. I wonder if he knows that I bought it back from the jeweler Rick had hocked it to. Or at least, I paid for about half of it. I don't know who made the final payment for me. I'm still mad when I think about how Rick stole my Forever ID bracelet from me.

The only good part about seeing Rick is that his hanging out with a bunch of really strong Christians seems to be having a good influence on him. I'm glad for that.

The strange part was that I didn't really feel anything deep inside when I saw him. I mean, I felt a little nervous, but I didn't feel all thrilled and eager for his attention the way I used to. How can feelings change like that?

One thing that didn't change this Thanksgiving vacation was my friendship with Katie. It was challenged a few times on this ski trip, but we ended up coming out of the experience much closer than we've ever been. I learned a lot about trusting the right people. Katie needed me to believe her and to be on her side when some other girls on the trip were trying to get me to take their side against Katie. I didn't stick up for Katie at first; at least, not the way she wanted me to side with her. I wish I had. All I can say is that I'm glad she's so forgiving and such a gracious friend.

Christy + Katie = "BFF!"
Best friends forever

The other big event on this ski trip was that I ran into the ski instructor. Yes, literally ran into him. I still can't believe I'm such a klutz sometimes. I think I'd like to try skiing again, only I'd like to go at my own pace without a lot of other people I know watching me. It was fun. I guess.

# November 30

Guess what I have, DSFriend?

A coconut from Hawaii! You should see it. Todd mailed me a coconut, and he wrote a Bible reference on it. He wrote "Phil.1:7." The man at the post office told me I got something from "Phil," and I said I didn't know anyone named Phil. It was so funny. Katie was with me, and we cracked up. The verse is in Philippians, you see. It says, "I hold you in my heart."

Is that the most romantic thing you've ever heard? Here I thought Todd was long gone, and he sends me a coconut and tells me in a secret, romantic, and holy language that he's thinking of me. Todd holds me in his heart. Ahh. I hold him in my heart, too. But then, you knew that, didn't you?

# January 16

I missed you, Dear Silent Friend!

My family went to the mountains with Uncle Bob and Aunt Marti for Christmas, and I wish I had taken you with me. I did a lot of thinking and reflecting, and if you'd been with me, you could have held those thoughts for me.

Two weeks have passed since then, and I'm afraid I've forgotten some of the things I was thinking.

I just can't believe we're already two weeks into this new year. All my teachers are giving us homework like crazy! I have a paper due for history on Friday, and I haven't started it yet. I ended up working extra hours last week at the pet store, and as soon as I got home, I just crashed. My room is a mess. I don't like being this far behind in homework or this unorganized.

Now for the big news, the reason I've been so busy. Todd is back from Hawaii! He came back on New Year's Day and showed up at my aunt and uncle's party with leis and hugs for everyone. He had some pretty fantastic tales to tell about his adventures.

We've seen each other three times since he came back, and I think all my old feelings for him are as strong as ever. His birthday was two days ago. I made him a big batch of chocolate chip cookies and bought him a gift certificate at a sports store where they have stuff for skateboards because he said his skateboard needed new wheels. It was a good choice. He seemed to really like it.

For his birthday we went to see this exhibit in Laguna Beach, which isn't far from where he lives. They had a big display of all these old surfboards and other California beach memorabilia from the '60s. One of the old wooden surfboards had been made into a bench, which Todd thought was very cool. It wasn't especially comfortable, but I agreed it did look pretty cool in the corner where they had it under a fake palm tree with a set of bongo drums.

My mom was really nice. She drove me up there and went to dinner with Aunt Marti while Todd and I went to the exhibit. Then we all had birthday cake at Bob and Marti's, and my mom drove me home. I would have loved to have stayed longer, but I'm happy that I could be with Todd on his birthday. I think it was one of the funniest times Todd and I have ever had. And I wouldn't be surprised if the next time I see him he tells me that he has turned his old surfboard, "Naranja," into a bench like the one we saw!

## February 1

I need a new pair of shoes, DSF.

Aren't you glad I told you? I only have one pair that I really like to wear, and they're coming apart on the side. I saw a pair I like, but I didn't even try them on because they were too expensive. Now I have to decide if I want to try to find another pair, or if I should keep checking on this pair and wait for them to go on sale. If they went on sale for 60 percent off, I could afford them. But what are the chances of their being marked down that much, especially in the next few weeks? I know. I'm dreaming. I need to face reality and go find another pair.

Now, if I asked Aunt Marti to get them for me I know she would, and the price wouldn't even make her blink. But I don't feel right about that. I know Marti likes to buy clothes for me, and she never acts as if it's a burden.

I just don't know how that makes my mom feel when Marti can afford to buy things that my parents can't. It's more important to me that I be a good caretaker of the things I have than to collect more stuff. My parents have taught me that. My dad fixes things when they break rather than going out and buying new ones to replace them. My mom has fewer clothes than anyone I know, but she always looks nice and she never complains. I think there's a sort of dignity that comes with making do with whatever you have.

But I still definitely need a new pair of shoes. Definitely.

## April 4

Do you hear the wind, DSF?

It's been stormy for five days now. Wet and cold and gray. We used to have spring days like this in Wisconsin, but I don't remember having this much rain since we moved here. It's kind of depressing.

## May 28

Hello, DSF,

My life has been full of school, church, work, friends. Sorry I haven't checked in with you more. Yesterday was Katie's birthday, and we had a huge party at this pizza place called Sam's. I planned it as a surprise and invited everyone I could think of from school and church. I told Katie I wanted to take her out for her birthday and that it would be my treat but all I could afford was Sam's. I don't know if she was suspicious or not, but she went along without any complaints.

When we arrived there, I told her I wanted to see something in the back room. She followed me in, and everyone jumped up and said surprise. It was great!

We had a gummy worm fight with this bag of gummy worms one of the guys brought. We threw those wiggly worms all over the place. One landed in my hair, and one slid down Katie's shirt. The gross ones were the ones the guys licked to make them stick on the wall and then picked them up again and threw them at people.

Todd and Doug came. They said they tried to talk Rick into coming, but he had a date. Are we surprised? Todd, Doug, and Rick are all roommates in San Diego. Yes, that one is surprising. A person never knows which relationships are going to come back around again.

## June 11

Dear Friend of Silence,

Tomorrow is the last day of school. My junior year went by way too fast! I think it was my hardest year as far as the amount of homework and trying to balance school and job and friends and everything. I'm feeling real melancholy tonight. It's like something is missing because I don't have anything to look forward to this summer.

Two summers ago I came to California to stay with Bob and Marti. Last summer Paula came, and we ended up going to Maui. But this summer absolutely nothing is on the schedule. Not even a family vacation. And who knows how much I'll get to see Todd since he said he's going to be working and maybe taking a summer school class.

Katie wants to go to camp with the church youth group. I think that's sounding more and more like a good idea. I'm going to talk to Luke about it to see if I can still sign up.

My brother is playing Little League baseball, and he made a two-base hit last week. I think it was the highlight of his life. David is still a pest, but the older he gets the more tolerable he is. I think he might turn into a fairly nice kid by the time he gets to high school. However, by then I'll be off to college, and I won't see him much. Isn't it funny that I'm even thinking of that now? And that I'm feeling sad about not being around my brother when he's in high school? I told you I was feeling melancholy.

# July 10

DSF, will you remind me to get more details from Katie next time she asks me to do *anything*?

I can't believe this. Katie talked me into going to camp, but now she's not going. The worst part is that I thought we were going to be the *campers* when she dreamed up this event. But no, she signed us up to be *counselors*! So yours truly is going to be a camp counselor, and Katie Weldon, the big flake, is staying home.

Actually, it's not her fault. And she's really not a flake. Her parents are funny about Katie being involved in a lot of church activities. When they found out the camp was a church camp, they didn't want her to go. I admire her for honoring her parents' decision even when it seems like an unfair and pointless one. Katie has more patience than I think I would have under the same circumstances.

The thing is, when Katie submits herself to her parents' decisions, I've seen God do His "God-things" in her life. (That's what Katie calls it when things happen you can't explain, but you look back at them, and all you can say is that God did it. That's why it's a God-thing.) And God blesses Katie in a special way for her obedience. That's why I can't be too frustrated with her for backing out of camp. It's not exactly her choice or her fault, and I want to support her in her decision even when it's difficult for me.

## July 21

Back from Camp Wildwood, DSF,

You should have been there! Actually, I'm glad I didn't take you. The girls in my cabin would have discovered you the first day, read all my secrets on your pages, and then tortured me the rest of the week. Yes, it's good that you stayed home.

It was an "interesting" week. That's the only word that comes to mind when I try to describe it. I learned that I'm not exactly the camp counselor type, although I was much better at it by the end of the week than I was the first few days.

I also learned that red ant bites are about the most torturous of all experiences. A whole army of red ants attacked me the last day when I hid inside a hollowed-out tree stump for the camp counselor hunt. My legs were covered with bites. And I mean covered. It was awful. I spent the last night in the infirmary.

My favorite song from camp was one I had heard before. Doug and Todd sang it when Katie and I visited their God Lovers Bible Study in San Diego a few weeks ago. It's from a verse in the Bible:

> Eye has not seen
> Ear has not heard
> Neither has it entered the heart of man
> The things God has prepared
> For those who love Him.

## July 23

Dear SF,

Katie called while I was writing my last entry, and then I had to go to work, so I never finished. I wanted to write more about camp because some good things happened there. The best of all was that Sara came to visit me in the infirmary, and she said she wanted to give her heart to the Lord. Here I'd been trying to "preach" to these girls all week and thought I'd failed. Then little Sara decides she wants to become a Christian, and she comes to the infirmary to ask me. It was amazing.

The other amazing thing was what I learned about myself with guys. I know, I talk about guys all the time, don't I? I don't think of myself as being boy-crazy or any-thing. It's just that I'm learning. As I go along, I want to remember what I've learned so I don't keep repeating the same mistakes—the sort of mistake I made at camp with Jaeson.

I spent way too much time focusing on him and playing out the role of being his summer camp crush. It wasn't terrible or anything. The canoe ride he took me on was fun and memorable.

What I learned is that I'm so open to whatever comes my way that some stuff comes rushing into my life, and I don't discern at the moment if it's a good thing or not. I don't decide ahead of time what I want or what's important. I mostly let things happen, and then I evaluate them later. I guess that's what I'm doing now.

And my evaluation is that I should have realized at the beginning of the week Jaeson was the kind of guy who had a different girlfriend every week. When he showed interest in me, I was simply his choice for a girlfriend for that week. If I'd realized that, I probably would have still hung out with him and gone on the canoe ride and everything, but I wouldn't have gobbled up the attention as if it actually meant something to him.

Does that make sense? It's like it's okay to develop

short-term friendships as long as I realize at the beginning that it's just a blip on the screen of my life. I don't need to make such a big deal of everything.

My mom wants me to help her fix dinner tonight, so I better go. She says I don't know how to cook, and it's time I learned a few things before I grow up and leave home. She says if I had to move out now, all I'd know how to fix would be scrambled eggs and toast. I didn't tell her this, but the scrambled eggs reminded me of when I made breakfast for Todd on the beach and the sea gulls scarfed them all up. I think it's about time Todd and I tried another breakfast on the beach. This time we'll keep the birds away.

# August 12

Greetings on a very hot night, DSF!

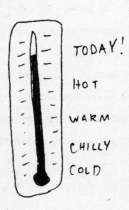

TODAY!

HOT

WARM

CHILLY

COLD

I have a fan blowing on me right now, but it's still so hot in my room that I don't know if I'll be able to sleep. The weatherman said on the news tonight that we broke a record yesterday and today for high temperatures. On the news they said the last time it was this hot in Escondido in August was in

1934 or something like that. My hand is sticking to the pages as I write this. Yuck! It's too hot!

My aunt has planned an end-of-the-summer outing. She and my uncle rented a houseboat at Lake Shasta, and we're going in a week and a half. Todd is coming! So are Katie and Doug. This is going to be the best trip ever. I have to admit I do love being spoiled by my aunt. She really gets into planning my social life for me, and even though it bugs me sometimes, I realize what a treat it is to be able to go fun places and do fun things like this with my friends.

Todd called last night. I was saying how the future seems like such a mystery. I'm about to begin my senior year of high school, and I can't figure out how I got to this last year so fast. Todd is about to start his sophomore year of college, and he needs to make some solid decisions about classes and his major.

Todd said, "I'm glad that God has plans even when we don't. God is 'prior.' Wherever we're going, He's already been there."

I liked that. God is "prior." He's already been there. He has charted a path for us to follow. The dearest desire of my heart is that I stay on that path and not go off on my own trail and waste any of my life on a trail that's not God's first and best choice for me.

## September 4

I only have a minute, DSF,

But I had to tell you my wonderful news. Todd and I are officially going together. We had this very romantic talk our first morning at Lake Shasta, and we decided the next step for us was to be a couple and to start going together. It's been sooooo wonderful!

He's coming this weekend to take me out. I can't wait to see him. We had such a great time on the houseboat. He is so amazing. I care about him more than I can say. We've come so far and waited so long to be at this next level in our relationship. I don't think I've ever been happier. I think Todd is happy, too. I feel as if our relationship gets stronger the more we each grow closer to God. Isn't that amazing?

I was trying to explain it the other day to my mom, but I didn't have the right words. It's a lovely mystery.

Today is the first day of my senior year, and I have to hurry. Katie and I are riding together, and you know how Katie doesn't like to wait for anything.

Christy + Todd    TA
True Love Always ??

## September 8

DSF,

I'm so worried about Katie. We met this guy, an exchange student from Ireland, the first day of school, and I think she's fallen for him in a big way.

## September 17

Katie and Michael are together now. I don't feel good about this. Todd and I met them at the movies last week. We all went together and then out for pie afterward. I really don't think Michael is a believer. What is Katie thinking?

## September 28

Hi there, Dear Silent Friend,

We celebrated my dad's birthday today, and I bought him a flashlight. I know. It sounds like a really dull present, but he liked it. Todd suggested I give my dad a personal card, so I ended up writing out the assignment I did for English in which I described my dad. He read it and teared up. Then my mom started to cry, and I got all teary-eyed, too. Todd was right. He said that dads like to hear every now and then that they're doing something right. My dad really liked it.

It made me think about my heavenly Father. I don't often tell Him how I feel about Him. I know He loves me, even though I don't think I'll ever understand how much. And I love Him, even though I don't think I'll ever be able to fully tell Him how much.

Heavenly Father,

I want to take the time now to tell you how much I love you. It's not enough just to realize that I don't tell you. I need to tell you. You are awesome, God. You have created the heavens and the earth and all that is in them, and yet you care about people, as small as we are. You care about what happens to us, and more than that, you want to have a relationship with us.

Thank you, God, for seeking me out and pursuing a relationship with me. I love you. I look back on my life and see so many times when you were at work doing your God-thing, even though at the time I didn't recognize what was going on. You have done so much for me.

Thank you. I love the way you comfort me and give me your peace in rough times. You provide for all my needs and many of my wishes . . . sometimes even before I wish them. It's amazing to me that you care so much about me.

Thank you very much, Lord. Thank you.

# October 4

Do you like your new shelf, DSFriend?

Can you still smell the fresh paint? It's supposed to be dry, but when I came in my room after the door had been closed all day I could smell the paint. I bought your new bookshelf at a yard sale last week, and Todd helped me paint it at Bob and Marti's house. It fits perfectly in the corner of my room. Every time I look at it I feel warm and content inside. Just a few minutes ago I was remembering the silly paintbrush fight Todd and I had while we were painting it. See my face? I'm smiling at the memory.

Things are so great with Todd. He is such an amazing guy. Sometimes I feel as if my heart is so full of appreciation and admiration for him that if I added one more pinch, my heart would burst. Sometimes I wonder if this is love. How do you know if you're really in love? How much of our feelings are we supposed to figure out and how much are we just supposed to feel?

I feel deliriously happy tonight. Happy to be alive and well. God seems so close right now. When we were on the houseboat trip, Todd and I went out in the raft the first morning and the sky was so beautiful. Todd quoted this verse from Nahum, "The clouds are the dust of His feet."

Now whenever I look up and see fluffy clouds, I think that God has been walking across the skies.

A few months ago we had a guest speaker at church, and he taught on a verse that says the Spirit of God roams the face of the earth looking for just one person who will be obedient and faithful to Him.

That's what I think of when I see the clouds. The Spirit of God is roaming the earth again, seeking the few who love Him above all else. I want to be one of those few obedient, faithful God-lovers. I feel as if I have so far to go and so much to learn. I want not only to read my Bible but also to study it more. I want to grow deeper in my relationship with the Lord so that when He speaks in His still, small whisper I'll be listening.

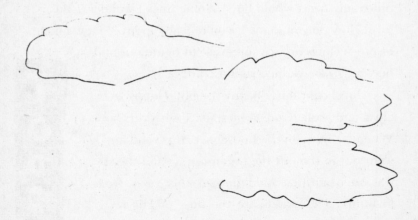

# January 6

I'm sorry, DSF,

I have neglected you. How long has it been since I slipped between your covers? Three months? I've missed you.

I can't catch you up on everything, but I do want to write down a few "markers" so I'll remember this season of my life. My senior year has been full so far!

Katie and I have gone through our biggest testing ever. Katie still has her boyfriend, Michael. And she's changed. A lot. I feel as if she and I are miles apart. I've been sooooo busy with school, work, church, Todd, and my family that I haven't put enough effort into keeping close with Katie. We had such a fantastic friendship. I don't want to let it go.

Todd has been telling me all along to pray for Katie, and I have been, but I don't see anything changing. She and Michael keep getting closer, and she and I keep moving further and further apart. It's depressing.

Todd's birthday is coming up on the 14th, and I don't know what to buy him. He and I have talked about what to do, but nothing seems to be working out. That's depressing me, too. I don't want his birthday to slip by without us doing something memorable.

The other thing I want to write down so I remember is that I've been enjoying being on the yearbook staff and taking pictures. It's a lot of work and a lot of hassle, and this guy Fred drives me crazy. But all in all, I like it.

## May 13

Dearest Silent Friend, I'm so glad I can talk to you.

I just spent the last hour or so reading all through this diary, and I'm amazed at how my life has changed. So much has happened. I'm glad you've been there for me all these years. You may be silent, but when I go back to read all these secrets you've held for me, it's as if you're speaking to the deep corners of my heart. I see God at work in my life.

And tonight I needed to see that. I did something today that I think I'll end up regretting or at least second-guessing for a long time.

I broke up with Todd.

I can't believe I'm just sitting here, telling you this, and that I'm not falling apart. I feel numb.

My reason for breaking up with him was quite noble, actually. Todd received an invitation to go on an extended missions outreach with a group he had contacted some time ago. It's what he's always wanted to do. And he wasn't going to go because we're together now and things have been so great. That's why I had to be the one to break up, to let him go. I don't think he would have done it.

I gave him back the Forever bracelet while we were at the beach watching the sunset. He crumbled to the sand and cried. He cried, DSF! I can't begin to tell you how I feel right now. See these teardrops? They're mine. And they're only the beginning.

We barely talked on the ride home. And then he walked me to the door, turned, and left. No farewell kiss, no wishes for our future. Just good-bye!

Oh, what have I done? What was I thinking? I felt so sure this was what God wanted me to do. But why? And if it was what God truly wanted, would it hurt this much?

I feel exhausted. I want to tell you more, but I can't right now.

*Forever . . .*

## June 24

I'm writing this with a hesitant hand, DSF.

I'm not sure I trust myself to write out my feelings at the moment. They've been so mixed up the past few weeks.

Todd has left.

He never called. Never said a special good-bye. He just left. Sometimes I'm sure I did the right thing. Other times, like right now, I ache, thinking that I made the biggest mistake of my life. I've plotted a hundred ways to get him back, but I haven't followed through on any of my schemes.

This whole phase of our lives feels bigger than I am. Bigger than both of us. It's as if this is about something else. A test maybe? Does God test us to see if we really mean it when we tell Him we love Him more than anything or anyone else? Or is it a self-inflicted torture that didn't need to happen? I mean, did I really hear God? Or in a deep, unidentified way, did I want to let Todd go? Was I feeling panicked about getting too close or about being too absorbed with him when I have all these other life-changing decisions to make, like where am I going to go to college in the fall? What do I want to be when I grow up?

I don't know. I'm second-guessing myself on everything. I freak out for a while, and then I have this calming peace, and I know God is still in control. Let me remind myself of that again.

GOD IS IN CONTROL!

He still has a plan He's working out. He's still "prior" to anything I decide or anything I do. He's God.

The most confusing element of this is Doug. He's suddenly in my life in a big way, as if he can step in to take Todd's place. I appreciate all the kind attention, but I can't figure out what is going on with him.

I have to go to work. I'll scatter all the rest of my insecurities across another one of your pages in a day or two. You can hold them for me, if you don't mind. Then maybe someday I'll come back to read these crazy words, and it will make sense. Or maybe it still won't make sense. But at least I'll know that in the midst of it all I was trying to trust God. Trying to understand and do the right thing.

## *June 26*

Hello there, DSF!

I imagine after the last few entries you might have thought I'd never have another happy word to write. But today I do. Katie and I went to the beach this afternoon, just the two of us, and we had the best time! She broke up with Michael a couple of months ago. I never told you, did I? It was around the same time I was breaking up with Todd, and I guess that took first place over Katie's broken heart.

*I'm TRYING, GOD!*

She and I call ourselves the "widow-women," and that allows us to treat ourselves to afternoons at the beach and to movies we both can cry at with an extra large tub of buttered popcorn between us.

Next weekend my family is flying back to Wisconsin for my grandparents' fiftieth wedding anniversary. It's the first vacation we've taken together in a long time. I'm looking forward to it. The only thing I'm not looking forward to is the possibility of seeing Paula. I haven't had any communication with her for so long. It's going to be strange to see her again.

## July 3

Dear SF,

What is love? How does a person know if she is truly in love? What makes love last? I think it's important to think through some of these things and to decide what's a priority to me.

Tonight my grandparents celebrated their fiftieth wedding anniversary at the church I grew up attending. I asked them how they knew they were in love and how they knew who was the right person to marry. They gave me several answers. Grandma says love is a one-time decision followed by lots of everyday small choices that build on that original decision. Grandpa was kind of funny. He said it has to do with what you have in common.

Here are two words I want to think about when it comes to relationships: commitment and intimacy. I think commitment needs to be the foundation for any lasting relationship. Just like I didn't have a deep and growing relationship with Christ until I first made a commitment to Him. With intimacy I think of knowing the other person's heart in a special way so that you share and treasure the same things that are important to him.

I never realized it before, but I want more of that kind of intimacy with the Lord. I want to share and treasure the things that are important to Him. I want to know what's in His heart.

And I know God wants that kind of intimacy with me. He knows everything I've tucked away in the secret corner of my heart, and He wants to share it with me.

Wow! I just had one of those moments in which everything seemed clear. I realized Almighty God has chosen to be committed and intimate with me. Love is a choice, just like Grandma said. And God chose to love me. Not just one time, but over and over again—even when I do things He can't stand. God chose me, and He chooses me every day. That's amazing.

## July 6

Greetings, my Silent One,

We're back from Wisconsin already, and I wanted to write about something that happened there. I didn't see Paula, but I did see Matthew Kingsley. He's a boy I grew up with and had a huge crush on all through elementary school. Matt came to see me the day we arrived at my grandparents'. After that, he and I spent a lot of time together and talked a lot. We both were trying to figure out if we had anything left of our childhood crushes. He always knew I had a crush on him, but this weekend I found out he had a bit of a crush on me, too.

We talked about our feelings and thoughts openly, which I thought was great. We decided, even though we feel a little something for each other, that doesn't mean we have to act on it. We were childhood friends, and now we can be old friends, moving into adulthood at a distance.

It was all wise and mature and nice. But now that I'm home, I'm having these funny little waves of second thoughts. I mean, what if a long-distance romance could have budded if we had encouraged it along?

I've been thinking about it a lot today, and I guess my conclusion is that when we walk with the Lord and trust Him along the way, He makes our path clear. If something was supposed to start up between Matt and me, then I believe God would have worked it out. I didn't miss any important clue along the way.

Do you want to know something I just thought of? I think I'm stuck in a pattern of "summer love." Ever since I met Todd on the beach the summer I turned fifteen, I've subconsciously looked for a summer romance each year. The summer I turned sixteen was when we went to Maui, and I was expecting much more "romance" from Todd. The next summer I was a counselor at camp, and I soaked up every bit of attention from Jaeson, as if that was supposed to be my heart fling for that summer.

This summer I'm "single," so, of course, I was expecting something poetic to spring up from being reunited with Matthew. This could be a dangerous pattern.

The funny thing is I have to stop writing this now because I can hear Doug at the front door talking to my dad. Doug and I are going to a concert at my church tonight. Here I am scanning the list of potential candidates for a summer romance, when a really "awesome" guy is waiting for me in the living room right this minute!

# July 31

Oh, my peculiar treasure, my Dear Silent Friend,

I've been crying for the last hour. You can't imagine how deeply I've been hurting all day. If a heart can bleed, I know mine is bleeding right now.

I turned eighteen on Tuesday, and everything was wonderful. Then today I was looking for something in my top drawer, and I found a picture of Todd and me and I just started to cry. Doug had taken the picture of us at Disneyland last summer when we were on the canoe ride. I had put it in a heart-shaped frame that Todd bought for me at Disneyland because he said he wanted to buy something special for me. When we were in the gift shop, Todd said, "Do you see anything else you can't live without?" and I said, "Yes. You." Todd said, "You could live without me, Christy." And I said, "But I wouldn't want to."

That's when Todd took my face in his hands and kissed me while we stood in the middle of the gift shop. There was a tear in his eye. He held me tight and whispered, "If you only knew, Kilikina. If you only knew." (Kilikina is the Hawaiian name Todd gave me.)

I didn't know what he was talking about, and I remember feeling panicky, as if something was wrong. Todd and I went on a long ride on the river paddle boat, and we talked under the stars. He told me about his childhood and how I was the first person who cared so deeply and consistently for him.

Now I'm crying again as I remember his face. It was only a year ago, but it feels like a lifetime. I've been lying here on my bed, looking at this picture and thinking that if what Todd and I had was only for a season, it was worth all the ups and downs and all the joys and aches. Knowing Todd Spencer was a precious, peculiar gift from God. I guess I wanted it to last forever, just like the inscription on the bracelet he gave me.

But even that bracelet is gone now, too. Todd has it. Or maybe he's sold it or given it to someone else. I have no way of knowing. He doesn't write to any of us from the old gang.

Doug is coming over tonight, and he's taking me out to dinner as a belated celebration for my birthday. Doug is such a good friend. I appreciate him. We just hang out together and talk. He doesn't mind if I talk about Todd. Sometimes I remember fun things Todd and I did. Doug jumps in and tells me stories of funny things that happened when he was hanging out with Todd before I met either of them.

Okay, I've stopped crying now. I think I needed to have one final good-bye cry over Todd. Now I need to put away all my memories of him so I can move on. The torture for me is wondering if he's thinking of me. Did he forget about me right away? Has he met someone else? Does he ever sit and look at an old picture of me and cry a little, too?

I guess I'll never know.

A few days ago I was reading in 2 Samuel 12 about how King David was in deep mourning when his baby was sick and dying. Then, when the child died, he got up, washed his face, went out, and worshiped God. Everyone asked why he went back to life as usual after being so upset.

I underlined what David said. I'll write it here for you. I know it doesn't exactly apply to Todd and me, but it helped me a lot.

"Can I bring him back again?

I will go to him, but he will not return to me."

I know David meant that one day he would go to heaven and be with his child, but the baby couldn't come back to earth to be with him. It helped me to think that I can't do anything to bring Todd back into my world, but we'll be together forever in heaven. I find a strange peace and hope in that promise of God's.

forever...

All I know is that I need to get up, wash my face, and go out with Doug tonight. Maybe it's time Doug and I talk about something other than Todd.

# August 7

You won't believe this, DSF,

Katie got a speeding ticket today! She had just dropped me off at home and was hurrying to get to her house before her favorite TV show started. (I don't remember the name of the show. I should since she keeps telling me to watch it, but I haven't seen it yet.) She was pulled over four blocks from her house, and she told the officer she was sorry and asked him to forgive her for breaking the law. Doesn't that sound like Katie?

She said he looked at her funny and said, "Apology accepted. I'm still writing you a ticket."

Then Katie said, "By all means, write the ticket. I deserve it. And I appreciate that you're making sure Escondido is a safe place for us to live and drive."

Then you won't believe what happened. The officer ordered her out of the car and made her take a drunk driving test! She passed, of course, and decided to stop trying to carry on a pleasant conversation with him. She took the ticket and got home in time to see the show's last ten minutes. Never a dull minute with Katie!

## December 1

Happy Thanksgiving, DSF!

Thanksgiving was actually last weekend, but I'm about a week behind on everything lately. When it comes to checking in with you, I'm more like a few months behind. The end of the summer zoomed by, and then I started classes at the community college. Life has been nonstop with work, homework, and Doug.

Doug and I are sort of going together now. About a month ago Doug and I had a long talk, and he said it would help him if he knew where he stood with me. I told him no other guys were in my life, and there hadn't been for many months. I think he had assumed I was hanging out more with the college group from my church since so many of them go to the same community college I do. I hang out with them all the time at school and on weekends, but I'm not especially close to any of the guys in the group.

So Doug asked if we should consider ourselves going together. It was hard for me to answer right away because all I could think about was Todd. I know. I need to stop that. But remember a year ago, when Todd and I had the same sort of conversation on the houseboat at Lake Shasta? Todd and I decided we wanted to take the next step of commitment in our relationship, which meant letting people know we were together.

It was so different when Doug and I talked about it. There wasn't anything romantic about it. We were in his truck's cab, sitting in the driveway, and my feet were cold because we had gone ice skating.

Doug is a great skater, and ice skating is about the only sport I can do sort of okay. We had so much fun! I think that's why Doug decided to have the "going together" conversation. Holding hands and skating together was a lot cozier than we usually get.

I pushed the warm memories of Todd away and told Doug yes.

Life can be strange and wonderful and mysterious all at the same time, don't you think?

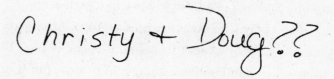

# December 11

Is this wacky or what, DSF?

We're going to England! Do you want to come, too? I'll bring you, I promise. Doug organized this short-term missions trip for a bunch of us. We're going in about a month. I have so much to do before then!

At this point it's Doug, Katie, Tracy, and me joining a larger group once we arrive. Some more people from the God Lovers Bible Study might end up coming. I'm so excited! Doug said we'll stay in an old castle in northern England for our training the first week. That part will definitely be a dream come true. I've always wanted to go to Europe, and I've always wanted to stay in a castle.

Doug told me about a school in Switzerland that's connected with an orphanage in Basel. I applied to go there last month, but I wasn't accepted. I was pretty disappointed, but then Doug found out about this mission in England, and he pulled the whole trip together.

One of my Christmas cards was returned to me today. It was the card I had sent to Alissa. Remember her? I had sent it to her grandmother's address in Boston, but it came back saying, "No longer at this address." I prayed for Alissa a long time today. I hope everything is going well in her life. The last time I heard from her was a year ago at Christmas, and I haven't been very good about writing to her, either.

I guess I shouldn't be so critical of Todd's never writing. I sent a Christmas card to his dad's address in Newport Beach. The card didn't come back, but I have no idea if Todd ever received it.

# January 8

Hold on to your hat, Dear Silent Friend!

The adventure begins. I'm on the plane now, between Doug and Katie, and we're flying to England. I still can't believe this. I feel as if everything in my life has been rushing past me these last few months, and I'm caught up in the current.

My dad was right in urging me to make some decisions about the future. I don't know what I want to be. I don't know if I like being grown-up. When did that happen, anyway? I must be grown-up if I'm on my way to England. I can't believe I'm in college. Sometimes I feel so independent, but other times I wish I could go back to simpler times when I would spend the whole day lying on the beach, doing nothing but watch Todd surf. Oops. I did it again; I mentioned the "T" word. I wasn't going to do that anymore. I know that

## January 10 or 11 (Not sure, exactly.)

I'm back, DSF, I got interrupted before, and I didn't want anyone "eavesdropping" on what I was telling you.

We're on a train to Lancashire, which is somewhere in northwest England. Everyone is asleep but me. I love the countryside, even though it's shrouded with a winter frost. I'm warm and cozy inside this comfortable train. If we make our connection in Manchester, we should arrive at Carnforth Hall before dinner and in time for the opening meeting of our outreach training.

How can I describe London? What a huge, ancient, modern, bustling, polite, quaint, crowded, exhausting city! Two days weren't enough to make its acquaintance. We did see the crown jewels at the Tower of London, like Katie wanted, and it was pretty interesting. But my favorite part was climbing to the top of St. Paul's Cathedral and looking down at the city. St. Paul's is such an incredible church. I've never been inside a huge church like that before, and it made me feel full of reverence and awe.

I found these words etched on stone at a church we visited in London. It was either St. Paul's or Westminster Abbey: "May God grant to the living, grace; to the departed, rest; to the church and the world, peace and concord; and to us sinners, eternal life."

## January 13

Dear Silent Friend,

Katie has been changing before my eyes. At first she was so impetuous about everything. Is that the right word? In London she seemed loud, determined, and kind of rude. But then she said she saw the way she was acting and wanted to change. And you know what? She did. She went from being freaked out about all the cultural changes to being open, intrigued, and eager to learn. I wish I could be that teachable.

A girl on our team is named Sierra. Isn't that a pretty name? I like it. I like her, too. She's every inch an individual and free spirit. It's funny how I'm always in awe of people who have that kind of personality. Katie and Sierra are both the kind of people who aren't afraid to show their emotions. I wish I could be more like them.

## January 14

Yes, I know what day it is, DSF.

And maybe that's why I just had to check in and tell you what I'm feeling. It's Todd's birthday, and I can't even send him a card because I

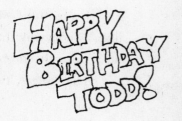

don't know where he is. Do you know it's been more than eight months since I last saw Todd or heard from him? It's like he has disappeared. I imagine he's in a jungle on some remote island. I can see him sleeping in a hammock every night, shaking coconuts from the trees for his breakfast, and loving every minute of it.

I miss him. But I'm happy for him that he's doing what he always wanted to do. At least I think I'm happy for him. I would probably be mad at him, too, for disappearing if my emotions weren't rather occupied at the moment.

I had a long talk with Doug on this little bridge on the grounds here at Carnforth Hall, and we both realized that we weren't supposed to be "together." I don't know why it took us so long to figure that out. There never was anything extra special between us. Sierra even suggested to Tracy that she and Doug would make a great pair, and Katie had to tell Sierra that Doug and I were going together! That's when I realized that if people didn't know we were together, then maybe we didn't want them to know for some reason. Maybe we were going through the motions, but our hearts weren't in it.

Doug said I was like a goal, but once he got me, he didn't know why that had been so important to him. That wasn't exactly what he said, but that's how I interpreted it.

The thing is, Tracy has liked Doug and has been waiting

patiently for him for a long time. They're together now, and that's as it should be.

So happy birthday, Todd, wherever you are.

# January 19

Do you feel the bumpety-bump of the train track, DSF?

We're on our way to Spain. Just you and me. Well, and Jesus, too. The mission director asked me at the last minute if I would go there. I don't know why I said yes. I was all set to go to Ireland with Katie, Doug, and Tracy.

I think I know what I'd like to be when I grow up. Or should I say, what I think God would like me to be when I grow up. I'd like to be a missionary. Here, in Europe. I like working with children. Surely there's some place that needs a missionary to tell the little kids about Jesus. Whatever it takes in schooling or training, I want to go after it wholeheartedly.

# January 20

I'm still here on the train, DSF.

It's been pretty scary traveling alone. I've felt Christ's presence closer than ever before, but I still feel a little unsure of everything. I've been looking in my Bible for a verse to call my own. That's what one of the guys on another team here told me to do. I like this one:

"We will not hide them from their children; we will tell the next generation the praiseworthy deeds of the LORD, his power, and the wonders he has done" (Psalm 78:4).

This one is good, too:

"Teach me your way, O LORD, and I will walk in your truth; give me an undivided heart, that I may fear your name. I will praise you, O Lord my God, with all my heart; I will glorify your name forever" (Psalm 86:11, 12).

Even though I don't know what lies ahead, I know I can trust God for whatever He has planned for me. And right now, that's as comforting as a thick blanket wrapped around me on this cold winter morning.

## January 22

Do you hear that, DSF?

It's a sound I'm beginning to love. It's the sound of the ocean breeze in the tall palm trees outside where I'm staying here in Castelldefels. It sounds like the trees are clapping. They've been clapping ever since I arrived at the train station. I wish you could have seen what happened. I know. You were zipped up inside my bag. Did you hear a certain deep voice call out, "Kilikina"? And did you hear me cry out with shock and joy, "Todd"?

Yes, Todd was here in Castelldefels! He's been here all along. Only I never knew that. The mission he joined is the same one I'm with on this short-term trip. They put Todd through leadership training and determined he would serve best here in Spain rather than on some island in a remote corner of the world.

Todd was late coming to meet me at the train, but he had a good excuse. He had a hard time finding the flowers he brought me—a big bouquet of white carnations, just like the ones he gave me the summer we met. I was so shocked, but he wasn't because he knew I was coming. The mission had sent him a fax.

He arrived with the carnations and a certain gold Forever ID bracelet, which he put back on my wrist. I'm wearing it right now, and it makes me smile just to look at it. So many memories. This is all such a huge God-thing that I think I'm still in shock.

I realized when I ran my finger over the engraved word, "Forever," on the bracelet, that the true forever part about this bracelet is not just Todd's promise to always be my friend. The real promise for forever is between God and me. Friends come and go. Life changes every day. But God promised He would never leave me. He never changes.

Jesus Christ is the same yesterday, today, and forever. I read that somewhere in my Bible.

Anyway, Todd and I rode in his very tiny car back to the mission house, and Todd introduced me to everyone. He kept saying, "This is Christy. My Christy. The one I told you about!"

Everything has been a wild blur since then. We only have four more days together, and then I go back to Carnforth Hall in England to meet up with the rest of the teams.

*Todd + Christy FOREVER!*

## January 25

My Dear SF,

Tomorrow I return to Carnforth Hall, and I'm a mess thinking about leaving Todd. I feel angry. Like, why did I get to see him again only for us to be torn apart once more? I don't understand.

# *February 4*

DSF,

Where should I jump in? How can I possibly summarize what's happened?

I'm back home in Escondido. Back from England. Back in classes at the community college. Back to my job at the pet store. Life is normal again. Only I'll never be normal because I've been to Europe. I saw God do amazing things. I got to be with Todd. And now I'm home, in my same room, on my same old bed with the same old bedspread, looking at the same dusty rose bookshelf Todd helped me paint so long ago.

What's going to happen now? I don't know.

Todd and I were able to squeeze in only one sort of long, heart-to-heart talk. We decided that we're back together. We both think it was a miracle that God brought us to the same place in Spain, and the whole time we were there, we were a great team. Our feelings for each other are as strong as they've ever been. Maybe stronger since we both know what it's like to be apart from each other for so long.

That's what we decided on the train from Spain back to England, when we had some time away from the rest of the team. Todd decided to travel back up to England with us, which was really, really wonderful because you know how distraught I was over saying good-bye in Castelldefels.

I have to run out the door, DSF. I'll finish later.

## February 11

Howdy, DSF!

A week and a half has passed since that last entry. Life is flying by at such a fast pace.

Let's see, where did I leave off on the Todd saga? Oh yeah. We decided we were going together again. I had the bracelet, we were happy, it all seemed great.

Then we went to the castle for the final few days of the conference. It was great fun to hear from all the other teams and to be together with Doug, Tracy, and Katie again. And do you remember Sierra? She fit into our group as if she had been with us from the start. It was really wonderful.

Our little group returned to London for a day before we flew out, and Todd came with us. I was so tired I ended up sleeping on his shoulder on the train ride all the way to London. We stayed at a boarding house near the Chelsea district. It's run by a woman who is associated with Carnforth Hall, so she was very gracious and didn't charge us anything to stay there. (But we left a good amount of money on the dresser for her.)

Anyway, when we got there, Todd and I took off by ourselves and walked for a long time, just holding hands, not saying anything. It was cold, but the sun broke through the clouds every once in a while. It wasn't as foggy as it had been when we were touring around a few weeks earlier.

When our fingers were finally too numb, we went into a bakery and sat in the back corner in a small booth. We ordered a pot of tea and some scones. It was kind of like the teatime I'd had with Tracy a few weeks earlier. Only this time Todd was sitting across from me. Never in a million years would I have pictured the two of us in London sharing tea. Our most exotic date yet!

We talked about our future, and I was the one who questioned how practical it was to say we were going together. I remembered some of the things I'd written here after my grandparents' anniversary, and commitment was the issue that kept coming up in our conversation.

I asked Todd how we could possibly be committed to each other when he was already committed to the mission for another year and a half. Then he said his commitment was really only for another month, and the mission director had announced it incorrectly at the last group meeting. That was a huge shock to me! They're restructuring things in Spain, and Todd was part of a temporary team that went there for the transition period. It's too long to tell you our whole conversation, but our final decision was to settle ourselves back into our regular routines and be committed to the things we'd already made commitments to. Then we'll pick up where we left off when Todd comes home. He might be home in a month, or he might be asked to stay another year.

Todd even had a verse for us to think about. (Typical, huh?) It's in Psalm 15 and talks about living a blameless life and how good it is to keep a promise, even when it hurts. It definitely hurts deep in my heart for us to be apart, but I see this as a chance to honor God and keep all my other promises at school, work, etc. And it hurts not to get to do what I want, which is, of course, to be with Todd.

At first I thought it would be impossible to go back to a normal schedule after being with him. But here I am, full speed ahead with school, work, church, and my family, and it actually feels okay. I don't ache over Todd the way I did before. It feels more like a long stretch between when we can be together. It's not a break-up, with the agony of wondering if we'll ever see each other again.

It's not great, mind you. But for now, I can do this.

## March 19

Dear Silent Friend,

I've just returned from a communion service at church. I didn't want to go at first because I was tired, but I'm so glad I did. They had a dramatization of the Last Supper. I got all choked up when they showed Jesus washing the disciples' feet. He demonstrated His love by serving.

That really struck me. I can love others the way Jesus loved them by serving them. I can make myself available to do even the most basic, servantlike tasks, and in that expression of serving, I will be loving others.

When we came home, I did the dishes without being asked, and then I took out the trash, which is usually my brother's job. I know those are minor things, but I felt so good about it because my heart was set on serving.

## April 2

Yippee, DSF!

Todd is coming home! That was fast, wasn't it? I really expected him to call and say he was staying another year. But he's coming home to finish school before making another long-term commitment to missions. He had been taking a correspondence course, but time got away from him. He never finished, so he didn't get any of the credit. He's planning to go back to a university near where his dad lives and try to click off some of the necessary units. He's been all over the place as a college student and is little more than halfway through what he needs to graduate. I wonder if this is a pattern in his life. Will he always take this long to finish projects?

He's on the plane right now and will arrive at LAX tomorrow morning. I can't miss class to meet him at the airport, but I hope to see him this weekend. I can't wait!

TODD'S COMING HOME!!!...

## April 12

Happy Easter, DSF,

What a week! I went up to Newport Beach, and Todd was waiting at my aunt and uncle's house. I ran to him when I saw him standing in the kitchen, and I'm not exaggerating when I say I threw my arms around him and burst into tears! I thought I was at the point in my life and in our relationship where I could control my emotions a little better, but I guess not! It was sooooo good to see him! This is only the second time I've seen him since he got back from Spain.

He is such a wonderful guy. I feel all warm and squishy inside just thinking about him now.

Unfortunately, the whole week wasn't warm and squishy. Sierra and her older sister, Tawni, came down, too, which was fun. But it made for a crowded, full week. I guess I'm more of an introvert than I realized. I like all my good friends, and I love spending time with them, but I'd dreamed up a different picture of the week. A picture that had just Todd and me in it, and everyone else faded into the background.

But I have to tell you, something very tragic happened. Uncle Bob tried to start up the barbecue, and it literally blew up on him. Todd burned his arm badly while trying to help Uncle Bob. My uncle ended up in the hospital, and his burns were serious. It was so scary.

My mom came up to be with Marti, and a lot of people from the God Lovers group showed up on the beach. Todd was in pain from the burn, but he did his best to act as if everything was fine. I kept reminding him to take his pain-killers, and he ended up irritated with me. It wasn't the best of times.

But I'll tell you what *was* the best of times. And this is a miracle. My uncle Bob did some soul searching while he was in the hospital, and he turned his life over to the Lord. I've prayed for this to happen for so long!

Bob had been going to a men's Bible study with Todd for a while, and Uncle Bob said the men from the group came to see him at the hospital. That's when he realized something was missing from his life.

The other big news is that Tracy and Doug are engaged! Doug asked her in such typically creative fashion. He hired an airplane to fly across the beach with a banner that read, "Tracy, will you marry me?"

Of course she said yes. I'm so happy for the two of them. They are great together.

I just reread the last few paragraphs. Does it sound like I made all this stuff up? My life is so bizarre sometimes! My uncle became a Christian; Doug and Tracy are getting married; Todd and I are on the same side of the planet. Yes, life is good. Or should I say, God is good. Very good.

Tracy, will you marry me

# July 23

Dear Silent Friend,

Oh, oh, oh, I am so sorry! Did you think I'd forgotten all about you? I put you in the zippered side pocket of my luggage when I went to Bob and Marti's over Easter vacation, and when I got home, I forgot to take you out. I thought I'd left you at their house, so I called Uncle Bob and asked him to look for you, but he said you weren't there.

Then I thought I left you in Todd's VW van, Gus. Now, there's a frightening thought! But when he came down a few weeks ago, I cleaned that filthy van for him in hopes of finding you, and you weren't there! I won't gross you out by telling you all the other things I did find.

I thought I'd lost you for good. I cleaned my room top to bottom twice and even put up a notice at school. I knew I'd never taken you to school, but I thought perhaps I'd left you in my backpack after a weekend trip to Newport Beach and then taken my backpack to school.

Please believe me when I say I was desperately sorrowful for having lost you. I felt as if a piece of my heart had been cut out and thrown away! I thought you were lost forever!

It's been months since I zipped you away in that side pouch. At least you were dry and warm there. I haven't used that bag since then. Until today. It's the middle of the summer, and I'm gathering my things to go to Bob and Marti's for the wedding of the decade (Tracy and Doug's, of course). And that's when I found you. I pulled the bag from the storage area, and when I did, I felt your edges through the side pocket. Were you trying to send me an SOS? You poor thing. I promise never to abandon you again like that.

Of course, I can't possibly catch you up on all that's happened since Easter in one little conversation, but let me tell you the most important news. I received a letter from a school in Switzerland, and I was accepted. Yes, Switzerland! I applied months and months ago, when Todd was long gone, and I didn't know where he was. I wasn't accepted then, so I pretty much forgot about the school. They offer work experience at an orphanage in Basel, Switzerland, so with the work experience combined with classes, it makes for quick course work.

Last semester I took seventeen units, but that was almost too much while working full time and helping in the nursery at church. Then Todd came home, and I suddenly had a social life again. Yes, seventeen units was definitely too much.

If I do go to Switzerland—and I haven't decided yet—I would be gone at least six months, maybe a year. My parents are all for it since apparently it's an honor to be accepted to this school. But I don't know if I want to go. I heard my mom talking to Marti about it, and I'm sure Marti was all for it.

I'll see Marti in three days. I'll see Todd then, too. This is a decision that needs a lot of prayer. As intrigued as I am with the delightful idea of returning to Europe, I don't know if I'm ready to be away on my own for such a long time.

## July 27

DSF, just a quick hello,

It's my birthday, and I can't believe I'm nineteen! I had a pretty good time with my family. My mom made a nice dinner, and we had some birthday cake, and I opened my presents. It was kind of mild, but so many other things are going on. Katie and I are going to my aunt and uncle's for Doug and Tracy's wedding tomorrow. That's why I didn't have a party or anything. Todd said he would come down for dinner, but I told him I wanted to have some time with my family. I'm hardly ever home anymore.

I think my dad appreciated that it was just the four of us. He likes Todd, but my dad has this funny idea that birthdays are supposed to be private and quiet instead of big celebrations. I like both at different times.

One of the reasons I told Todd he didn't have to come down was because he was here last weekend, and we were at a picnic with my parents' Sunday school class. Todd came for the day, and I thought he and I were going to go to the beach. But he found out about the picnic and said he would rather go with my parents.

So we went to the picnic, and he spent the whole afternoon hanging out with all these other families that he didn't even know, playing volleyball and even horseshoes, if you can believe that. I sat at a picnic table playing Scrabble with my mom and her friend. It was as if Todd and I hadn't even come together. When we left, he was so happy and thanked my parents for the fun day.

I thought about it a lot and decided that since Todd doesn't have much of a family, he probably didn't grow up going to family reunions, picnics, or camping trips. This is all new to him, and therefore it's fun. He has spent most of his life by himself or with his peers. Being around older, middle-aged, and young people all at the same place is a treat for him. Funny, huh?

# *July 29*

Dear Silent Friend,

I'm going to Switzerland. At least for a visit to the school. My ever-eager-to-run-my-life aunt Marti made arrangements to take me there to check out the school. She assumed Todd would go with us, but Todd decided to stay home because he didn't think he could get the time off work.

What's up with that? Since when did my boyfriend become responsible and dependable? Those are qualities I've always wanted in him, but why now, all of a sudden, when we could have gone to Switzerland together?

Katie couldn't go with me. That's a long story.

So I invited Sierra. Remember Sierra from the missions trip last year in England? I'm glad she was able to go. This is not a journey I wanted to make with just my aunt. Sierra is a lot of fun to be with, and she'll be good at helping me make the decision about whether to attend school there.

And yes, of course, I will take you with me. And I promise not to lock you in the side pocket of my bag. That's certainly the drawback of being a Dear "Silent" Friend. You can't call out and tell me where you are!

## August 7

*Ciao,* DSF!

I know. *Ciao* is Italian, and we've been in the German-speaking part of Switzerland. But it's the only foreign greeting I could think of at the moment, and everyone says it over here. We're on our way home already from Switzerland. Marti and Sierra are asleep, and most of the other passengers are watching the in-flight movie. I had intended to check in with you much sooner on this journey. But you know how it goes. Especially with my aunt. It was a rather stressful, nonstop few days. The bright spot was Sierra. If she hadn't been here, I don't know how crazy I might be by now.

So you want to know if you and I are going to be living in Switzerland for a while, do you? Well, the answer is, I think so. I want to pray about it some more, but I've pretty much decided this would be a very good thing in my life.

It's not as if I have to prove anything or take off and leave Todd simply because he took off and left me—more than once. It's that this is a rare opportunity. Sierra told me to put it in perspective, knowing that if I end up with Todd, we'll be together the rest of our lives. But I won't be able to pick up and move to Switzerland any time I want to. She said to picture myself as an old lady in a rocking chair after all my teeth have fallen out. That's when I'll be glad that when I was young and free, I took advantage of this opportunity.

So now we're flying home, and I have to find a way to tell Todd. Do you think it will be hard? Or will he be his nonchalant self and say, "Whatever you want"? That's pretty much how he acted when I told him about this opportunity. He said, "I'll pray that you make the right decision." Well, I hope he's still praying, and I hope this really is the right decision.

## *August 16*

Hi there, DSF!

It's all systems go for me to attend the school in Switzerland. Todd said pretty much the same thing Sierra and everyone else has been saying, that opportunities like this don't come along every day and that I'll be sorry if I don't take advantage of this chance.

I found a verse I'd underlined a long time ago in my Bible, and it gave me great peace and confidence that this was the way for me to go. It's in Psalm 107:29–31. "He stilled the storm to a whisper; the waves of the sea were hushed. They were glad when it grew calm, and he guided them to their desired haven. Let them give thanks to the LORD for his unfailing love."

I know this decision hasn't exactly been a "storm," but I've felt tossed back and forth during this past year as I've tried to decide about schooling and what I want to do with my life. Or should I say what God wants to do with my life? Then you throw Todd back into that "storm" after he was gone for so long, and it's been pretty unsettling.

I can't explain why, but this opportunity to go to Switzerland has turned into a calming decision. Like those verses, it's as if God has settled all my storming with one whisper, and He is guiding me to my desired haven. Not that I ever desired Switzerland, exactly. But the seas appear calm as I now sail off in that direction.

Things are peaceful with Todd. He has a few things to tend to in his life, such as finishing school, getting some money in the bank, and deciding what he wants to do after college.

I'm not worried about our relationship dissolving like I used to worry in the past. We talked about it, and Todd sees this as a season of planting for both of us. It's hard work to prepare a field and plant everything in neat rows. But now is the time to do that in both of our lives, and the planting can be done better if we're in separate corners of the world. Reaping the harvest will come later.

# August 23

Oh brother, DSF!

Did I sound mature and spiritual in that last entry or what? I'm glad I wrote all those thoughts down and that they were so clear then because they're definitely not clear now. This is going to be hard!

In our conversations during the past two days, Todd and I both have been hinting that this Switzerland decision is tougher than we thought. But neither one of us has said, "Maybe Switzerland isn't such a great idea after all." That's probably because we both know it's the right direction for me, even if we doubt how great it's going to be for our relationship.

Katie is the one who took it the hardest. She and I have been inseparable almost as long as Todd and I have, which is what, five years now? Unbelievable. Of course, Katie and I have had our ups and downs, too. But for the most part whenever we've been able to do something, we do it together. She wants to go to Rancho Corona, a private Christian college about an hour from here. I think it sounds like a great school, and I think she should go. She's not sure she wants to go until our junior year so I can go with her.

We had this huge discussion about Katie's taking the initiative to go to Rancho Corona by herself, and she blurted out that she was mad I hadn't talked through the Switzerland opportunity with her more thoroughly or sought her opinion about it. I didn't because everything happened pretty fast. So I told her I was sorry, and I asked her opinion. She said, "I think you should go."

I said, "What was that all about?" And she said, "I just wanted you to ask my opinion, as if it mattered to you. That's all."

So now I may be headed for my "desired haven" like those verses said, but believe me, the waters have not been calm and hushed.

## August 29

Oh, Dear Silent Friend,

It's been another night of good-byes. I'm at Bob and Marti's, and tomorrow Uncle Bob will drive me to LAX. I'll board a plane all by myself and wing my way to Switzerland. I still can't believe it's happening. Katie and Todd organized a going-away party tonight. Of course it was here at Newport Beach, and of course we all gathered around the fire pit and sang for hours. It was so wonderful! I can't begin to describe the torturous emotions I felt all night.

Doug and Tracy came. It was the first time I'd seen them since they got married, and they both had these happy smiles on their faces the whole time. They were adorable.

Katie cried off and on all night and told me it was as hard on her as it had probably been for me when Todd left. I don't feel the same intense sadness about leaving Katie. I actually thought tonight that this might be good for her, to have me gone for so long. She's such a people person. She needs to meet new people and get involved in new groups. She wouldn't do that if I were still around.

Todd cried a little, too, when we were saying good-bye on the patio. Everyone else had gone. He and I sat close on the low cement brick wall that faces the beach. For a while we just held each other and cried. We kissed three times. One for the past, he said, then one for the present, then a long, tender kiss for the future.

I'm crying again. I'll talk to you later, DSF. I can't write about this now.

# *September 25*

Hello from Switzerland, DSF!

I've been here three weeks, and I have to admit that every time I thought of writing about my experiences and feelings here on your pages, I ended up writing a letter instead. I've been keeping the computer in the library busy with all my emails to Katie, Todd, Uncle Bob, and Doug and Tracy. My parents don't have a computer. Can you believe that?

Uncle Bob was going to give me his old laptop before I came on this trip, but I told him I didn't need it. Boy, was I wrong! I may ask him to send it to me after all because it would sure help not to have to go to the library every time I do my homework or write to someone.

I've written so many details to everyone else about the school. I know I'll never forget this season of my life, so I don't know exactly what to tell you.

I like it here. The program is intense. The classes are good. Each time I go to the orphanage, it rips out my heart. So many children. So much pain. You can read the suffering in their little faces. In a modern world, you would think there wouldn't be so many abandoned children. You would think that refugees were from the last world war, not from the ongoing "conflicts" still plaguing parts of Europe. It's much harder to be around these children than I thought it would be. I'm learning a lot about myself and my ability to be compassionate.

# October 18

It's autumn, DSF,

And it's beautiful here.

I have two friends I hang out with at school, and they also happen to be my two roommates—Amelia and Sandra. They're both from Germany, but their English is perfect. They were friends before they came here, so they're being kind to let me join in with them.

Most of the students go to the bars on weekends. Amelia, Sandra, and I usually go for coffee or sometimes to the theater. The movies are in English, and you pay a different price depending on where you sit in the theater. They always sell out on Friday and Saturday, so you have to buy your ticket early.

I'm beginning to feel settled in, pretty much.

Todd sends me emails. Can you believe it? He apparently has been spending a lot of time at my aunt and uncle's house, and Uncle Bob lets Todd use his email account. It's really nice since he's never written to me before. Except for that coconut from Hawaii.

But email isn't the same as seeing his handwriting or touching the same sheet of writing paper that he touched. Does that sound silly? I'm never happy, am I? Todd is writing me several times a week. I should be happy, shouldn't I? Okay, I'll be happy and content with what I have, which is a lot.

## November 4

Happy *Langsam Samstag,* DSF!

That means "Long Saturday." In Basel, once a month, they have Langsam Samstag, and all the stores stay open longer so everyone goes shopping. It's kind of fun. Amelia and I went shopping for little necessities today. I stopped by a bakery that Aunt Marti, Sierra, and I had gone to last summer. I was told that every season the Swiss make different kinds of breads and cookies. I bought a fall wreath bread, and I just may eat the whole thing myself—it's that good!

Amelia talked me into buying some hot *Moroni* from the street vendors. Moroni are nuts. Chestnuts, I think. They roast them in a circular metal pan that looks like a big wok. You can smell the nuts a block away, and do they smell inviting! The vendors scoop the chestnuts into a cone-shaped bag, and you're supposed to walk and eat them while they're still warm.

Well, I don't know if I ever told you, but I hate nuts. I've always hated nuts.

That doesn't mean I haven't tried nuts of all kinds. The closest I came to liking them was when I tried macadamia nuts on my frozen yogurt in Maui. They were pretty good.

So I tried the Moroni. I didn't like them. I gave them an honest try, but I could only swallow one of them. Amelia ate all hers and the rest of mine.

## *November 11*

Dear Silent Friend,

Can you keep a secret? Although I guess it's not really that big a secret. Sandra has a boyfriend. They're pretty serious about each other. Amelia is sad, of course, because she doesn't have a special guy in her life. She and I have been doing nearly everything together.

I don't know how long we'll keep that up, though. Amelia and I have different interests. I'm just as content to stay in my room and read on weekends. Or go to the library and spend several hours catching up with my friends back home via the Internet.

Amelia likes to go and do and see. She loves to shop. I'm certain she and I have been in every store within a forty-kilometer radius of our school. I have bought, wrapped, and mailed all my Christmas presents for home, and now I have no desire to shop again for several weeks. But Amelia is making plans for our next shopping excursion, and I'm trying to decide how to tell her I don't want to go.

## November 19

Dearest Most Silent Friend,

Do you ever get tired of holding all these thoughts for me? I'm feeling very lonely today. I told Amelia I didn't want to go shopping with her last week, so she went with Jillian, a girl from Norway. Now Amelia and Jillian are inseparable, and I'm alone. I thought that's what I wanted. But it can be awfully depressing when the rest of the girls in the dorm are gone and I'm the only one left.

I'm still in my PJs. It's cold today, and I'm content to stay right here in my warm bed and visit with you. When I do convince myself to get out of bed, I'm going to bundle up, go to my favorite bakery, and buy something yummy. Then I'm heading for the library to check my emails and see if any of them are from Todd.

He doesn't write as often as he did when I first got here, but then I don't, either. He is taking fifteen units this semester and is working twenty hours a week at a hardware store in Newport Beach. In his last email he said they had had a big winter storm that kicked up the waves, so he was planning to go surfing early in the morning like he used to do in high school. It made me homesick. I wanted to go to the beach with him and make some scrambled eggs. Sigh.

## November 28

Gobble, gobble, DSF!

This afternoon the fourteen Americans who are at school here had a mock Thanksgiving dinner. I think we were all homesick and not as good company for each other as we should have been. We had deli sliced turkey, rolls, applesauce, and green beans. Some of the other students stopped by our corner of the lounge to figure out what we were doing. We tried to explain Thanksgiving.

All I could think of were Thanksgivings in the past. When I was six I got sick on the candied yams and went to bed in my grandparents' puffy bed. When I was ten we had so much snow that instead of driving the eight miles to my grandparents' house, we stayed home and had clam chowder with cheese and crackers. The electricity went out at my grandparents', so they couldn't cook the turkey until the next day. We ate it on Sunday after church, but it was pretty dried out.

I told one of my friends here about Thanksgiving weekend two years ago when Katie talked me into going skiing. Remember that adventure?

I wonder where I'll be next Thanksgiving. One thing I've learned is that God's ways aren't our ways and His thoughts aren't our thoughts. I could guess now where I'll be, but the future is really a mystery. A faith walk. And in my opinion, an adventure worth taking.

## December 7

Oh, man, is it cold here, Dear S Friend!

The snow is beautiful, but it's cold. I forgot what a winter with snow can be like. I had to buy some more socks yesterday, and they're a good pair. At least my feet are warm today.

The orphanage is warm enough, which is a good thing for all those children. The lecture hall at the school is drafty, and some students even bring blankets to put around themselves while they listen and take notes. I haven't robbed my bed yet, but I've considered it! Amelia thinks I have "thin blood." She says it in German with dramatic emphasis, and it sounds really funny.

Sandra and her boyfriend are still together. I can't pronounce his name, and I'm certain I couldn't guess how to spell it. Amelia and Sandra have been good roomies. They are hardly ever here, which is okay with me because I've enjoyed having the room to myself and being able to study.

It's a small room with one set of bunk beds and one bed against the opposite wall. I have the top bunk, which was a good choice because heat rises!

The work-study at the orphanage has been a great experience for me. It takes a lot out of me, but it's been good. One little boy, Tejas, was so shy when I first went there. He's been opening up slowly, and now he smiles when I come into the play area. I know that's a little thing, but he seems to have come far. I understand now why the school asked for a minimum commitment of six months. It would be too hard on the kids at the orphanage to have the workers change every few weeks. I'm pretty sure I'm going to stay through next summer. Although tonight, in this dark, chilly, quiet room, when I'm feeling so alone, next summer seems like a painfully long time off.

## December 12

Merry Christmas, DSF!

Christmas is two weeks away still, but I wanted to check in with you before all the craziness begins. My aunt sent me an early Christmas present, a ticket to fly home for two weeks during Christmas vacation. I wasn't expecting it. Now I'm excited to go home, but at the same time it feels like too much of a luxury.

You see, most of my friends here are going home, but they're just taking the train for a few hours so it's not such an expense. I was invited to go to Holland with Julia, one of the girls in another dorm whom I met a few weeks ago when she started to help out at the orphanage. I was looking forward to experiencing Christmas in another culture. But now I feel obligated to go home.

Don't get me wrong. I want to go home. I want to see everyone. It's just that I said all my huge good-byes in September because I thought I wouldn't see my U.S. friends and family for a year. Now I'm going to show up after only three and a half months.

But I'll see Todd. And I'm sure that will be wonderful. I've missed him in a deeper way than ever before. I think it's because I have tiny bits of him through the email now, when in the past, I had only silence if we were apart. Well, silence and one coconut.

# December 28

I'm home, DSF,

Do you recognize the familiar surroundings of this bedroom? Yes, it's ours. Isn't it strange being here? Katie has been over every day, Todd has been here five of the last seven days, and my mom keeps following me around, telling me all these little details of life that I've missed out on for the past few months.

I keep thinking of the kids back at the orphanage. Julia and I bought sweets for each of them as a Christmas gift. One little piece of candy per child is certainly not much, especially when I sit here with this mound of gifts, including a brand-new laptop from my uncle. I told him I was interested in borrowing his old one, but instead he bought me a new one. Too much. I don't need so much.

It's been sooooo stressful with Todd. I didn't think it would be like this. He's quieter than usual. Or maybe I've forgotten how quiet he can be. I tell stories about school and the orphanage, and he just sits there and listens without commenting. It makes me feel as if Switzerland is completely my experience and he's not attached to it in any way.

Katie has been the opposite. She's like my mom in that she has talked nonstop to bring me up to speed on every single thing that has happened since I left. Some of it doesn't interest me at all. Is that rude to say?

Katie's most exciting news is that she applied to Rancho Corona College, and she's going to start in January. I'm really happy for her. I think it will be wonderful.

Todd and I have plans to go to the mountains tomorrow. My brother wants to come, of course, and Katie heard us talking about it and volunteered to get a group together. Todd told both of them, "This is a day for just Christy and me."

David and Katie were both upset. I don't know how I feel. I'm eager to spend some time alone with Todd since we've been with people the whole time, but I don't like people being mad at me.

## December 29

Our snow day was a disaster, DSF!

Todd and I tried to get away this morning to go up to the mountains, but dear old Gus broke down about forty miles from my house. We spent the day waiting for a tow truck, then sitting in an automotive repair shop for almost five hours while they replaced the generator. Or was it the starter? I don't know. But Gus is back on the road now. We just sat there in that waiting room with all these other people, watching TV. Just sat there! Todd slept part of the time. I read magazines.

After Gus was fixed, we decided to get something to eat. I ordered a salad, and two little green worms were in it! After the waiter took it away, I couldn't eat anything else.

Todd drove me home, and we took my brother to the skate park. Todd and David went skateboarding for a couple of hours while I sat and watched them. Then we had dinner with my parents, and Todd went home.

What is happening to us? We're like two numb blobs! We can't go forward, and we can't go back. This trip home was a mistake. I don't belong here. Not now.

## *January 28*

It's cold, DSF,

The heater in our dorm room has been going on and off all week. We have three inches of snow on the ground, which makes this part of the Black Forest look enchanting. I have on several layers of clothes and am under my covers, but my nose is still cold!

You know, I've done so much writing on computers and my laptop that writing on your pages with a pen is sort of refreshing. It's a little slower and more calming.

# February 2

Not much to report, DSF,

I write all the news home in emails and spend the rest of my time writing papers. Life has become a pleasant routine again after the trip home for Christmas. It will be Valentine's Day in a few weeks. I've been thinking a lot about whether or not I should send Todd a card. I don't expect him to send me one. Writing letters and sending cards has never been his thing.

After all the time I spent with him at Christmas, things between us felt unsettled when I came back to school. I had a much better feeling in the fall that our relationship was going into a season of planting. At Christmas it felt as if I'd turned over dry earth to check on the seedlings I'd planted, but they all looked lifeless.

# April 4

Hello, my DSF,

I've been thinking about the analogy of the seeds in my last entry. It's been a little more than two months since I wrote that. The pace around here has left little time for reflection.

We had a break today, so I went for a hike up in the

hills where Sierra and I went with Alex when I was visiting the school last summer. I went with five other students who have become good buddies.

We're sort of the group of leftovers after so many others have paired up as boyfriends and girlfriends during the first half of the year. Julia, my friend from the Netherlands, was in our group, but about four weeks ago she and a Canadian guy decided they were more than friends and started doing things as a couple. So the unattached ones are dwindling in number.

I'm glad I haven't been interested in any guys here. It makes for such an intense experience.

Anyway, on our walk today the countryside was breathtaking. The snow is all gone. They say it melted early this year. And now the wild flowers are sprouting everywhere. It's so beautiful!

I picked a bunch of little yellow flowers, lacy white ones, and a few blue ones. I wish I knew their names. Tatiana teased me and said, "You don't know their names? I do. That's Marie, and this one is Peter."

She's so funny. She reminds me of Katie only with a South African accent. She's one of the few Christians here, and we've been going together to church since last November. It's a very small church, about a ten-minute walk from the dorm. The service is in English at 8:30 A.M., which is why Tatiana and I go there. The congregation is a unique mix of English-speaking people of varied ages. The minister is from Wales, and I love his accent.

Back to my story about the seedlings and feelings I'd dug up when I saw Todd at Christmas. I realized that if I'd taken a walk into these Swiss hills last December and turned up the earth, I wouldn't have found the delicate blue, yellow, and white wild flowers I found today. They would have been seeds. Tiny seeds, I'm sure. And they would have looked lifeless. It takes time and the miracle of God's resurrection power to bring anything back to life, including seeds and my deep feelings for Todd.

It's not exactly like my feelings for him are dead. It's more like they're buried for a season. That helps me to understand why things didn't feel all bright, colorful, and lively between us at Christmas. What we both seemed to be feeling was accurate for that season of our lives.

Putting our relationship in that perspective makes so much sense to me. And it makes me glad I wrote it out so I can come back here and look at this when I feel confused again, which I'm sure I will.

# *April 5*

This is so cool, DSF!

You know how yesterday I wrote all that stuff about understanding seeds looking lifeless when they're in the dormant season and how that's what it felt like with Todd at Christmas? Well, you'll never guess what the message was at church this morning. The pastor was speaking about how during Holy Week, between Palm Sunday and Easter, Christ tried to prepare the disciples for His death. (Palm Sunday is next week.) In John 12:23–28, Jesus told them, "I tell you the truth, unless a kernel of wheat falls to the ground and dies, it remains only a single seed. But if it dies, it produces many seeds."

I never noticed those verses before! Clearly this is God's design in so many areas. Seeds have to die before they sprout and produce a bountiful harvest. Christ had to die before God could raise Him from the dead and multiply that resurrection power in believers' lives over and over for thousands of years.

At the risk of over-spiritualizing my relationship with Todd (which, by the way, is something he has done since the day I met him so maybe it's okay if I do it every so often), in some ways our relationship had to die for God to demonstrate His resurrection power and bring new life to it. What I now understand is that when God brings new life, the harvest is abundant. One seed is designed to multiply its life after it dies to itself and is resurrected.

I'm not explaining this very well, but I understand it. Deep in the caverns of my heart I understand this. My life is not just to be lived to benefit myself or even to please one other person. When I die to myself and all that I consider precious or essential to my happiness, then God brings new life. When He does, it's multiplied to reach many.

I wish I could explain this better. I finally understand what it is I'm supposed to do with my life. My heart's desire is to die to myself and live to serve Christ so that He can multiply the results. It's like the last part of verse 26: "My Father will honor the one who serves me."

## May 6

Hello, Dear SF,

These past two weeks at the orphanage have been very difficult. About one-fourth of the children, the healthy ones who stood a good chance of being adopted, were transferred to another center in Austria. The others stayed. More than fifty new children are expected to arrive next week from Romania. This is so painful to watch. All these young hearts so eager and willing to love and to be loved.

All the children who were leaving were placed in a playroom. I was assigned to watch over them while the orphanage staff made the final arrangements and gathered the children's belongings.

You know what I did? I blessed each child. I went to each one, placed my hand on his or her forehead, and gave each one the blessing Todd gave me years ago. I looked it up in my Bible once. It's in Numbers 6:24. But it's different there than the way Todd said it to me. I seem to remember Todd's version, so this is what I said:

> May the Lord bless you and keep you.
> The Lord make His face to shine upon you
> and give you His peace.
> And may you always love Jesus first,
> above all else.

Very few of the children speak English. They had no idea what I was doing. But do you know, after I blessed the first two children and kissed them on the cheek, the others silently lined up, waiting for a blessing and a kiss.

All I could think of was when the disciples tried to send away the children, but Jesus stopped the men and said, "Let the little children come unto me . . . for the kingdom of God belongs to such as these."

Oh wow! I just looked up the reference for that verse.

It's Mark 10:14. And do you want to know what verse 16 says? "And he took the children in his arms, put his hands on them and blessed them." Jesus blessed them! He hugged them! That's what I did today.

It felt like such a tiny gift to give the children, but it's what I had in my heart to give. I did the same thing for those orphans today that Jesus did for the children who were being sent away from Him two thousand years ago. Amazing!

## May 14

Have you noticed, DSF?

You have only a few blank pages left. How can that be? It seems we've had endless room—my ink, your pages. But now our space is limited. I'm so sad. I feel as if every word from here on out must count.

I have only three more weeks of classes, and then we have a break for almost a month before the summer session begins. I've decided to stay through the summer because I can gain more transferable credits than if I went to summer school at home.

I've applied to Rancho Corona for the fall. Katie is already there this semester, and she's loving it. She said Sierra and some of her friends came to Rancho with Sierra's brother to visit the campus and to decide if they want to go there in the fall, too. It's possible that Katie, Todd, Sierra, and I will all be at the same school at the same time! Isn't that wild? I never would have imagined it.

I don't know what I'm going to do for my term break before summer session. I'd like to travel around, but I haven't made plans yet with any of the other students here. I guess I could travel by myself and just visit a dozen of my friends from school since they live all over Europe. But I don't like traveling by myself very much. I did it that one time from England to Spain, and that wasn't my favorite experience. It was good, but it was pretty faith stretching, too. The best part was the end of the journey when I saw Todd.

## *May 18*

DSF,

I'm so bummed out. I received a D on one of my papers for my critical analysis class. It's been my least favorite class, and I don't even think they have the same kind of class in the U.S. I didn't work very hard on my paper. It was only two pages, but it's the first D I've received. I could write the paper over, and the professor said he would average the new grade with the D, but I don't have time to work on it since all my other classes have papers and projects due in the next three weeks. Then we have a week of finals, and I'm through until the summer session.

## May 19

Guess what, Dear Silent One?

You'll never guess. I'm going to travel around Europe for three weeks during my break. And guess who is traveling with me? No, not anyone from here. Give up?

Katie and Todd!

Can you believe it?! My aunt once again is playing the role of the wealthy fairy godmother. She emailed me to ask about my plans for the break. I said I hadn't made any arrangements yet because I was so overwhelmed with my final projects, plus we have more children at the orphanage than at any other time since I've been here.

So dear Aunt Marti emailed me back and said, "Don't make any plans. All has been arranged." I thought she was going to buy me a ticket to fly home for a month the way she did at Christmas, and I was going to tell her no thanks. It was hard at Christmas to step in and out of that life and then in and out of this life. I didn't want to do that again when I only had the summer session and then I'd be home for good.

But then I received this screaming email from Katie. And I do mean screaming! She wrote the whole message in capital letters so it "sounded" as if she were shouting at me. She told me that Marti's surprise wasn't a ticket for me to come home, but two tickets to Switzerland—one for Katie and one for Todd. Of course, when I emailed Marti to thank her, she was upset Katie had spoiled all the fun of her surprise.

I called my parents and talked it through with them, and they're fine with the travel arrangements as long as Todd and I are always with Katie. They don't want Todd and me to go off by ourselves. My mom got kind of choked up when she said I was old enough to make my own important decisions and travel around, and she was proud of all that I'd accomplished this year.

Todd called yesterday, and he sounded excited about the trip. Of course, he already has plans to go to Spain to see his friends there. Katie emailed that she wants to go to Norway, and I decided that more than anything, I'd like to see all that I can in Italy. It's been a cold winter and spring, and I like the thought of sunny Italy.

Who knows if we'll come up with a compatible plan before they arrive on June 6. I checked out some maps and travel books from the library this afternoon. It's going to be difficult to concentrate on my studies while those travel books are sitting in the corner calling to me.

# June 5

Our last page, Dear Silent Friend,

I'm so sad. You have been my Dear Silent Friend for almost five years. Todd and Katie arrive tomorrow. I had planned to go into Basel and buy a "sister" diary to take along on our travels, but I didn't get to it. You won't be too jealous, will you, if I share my jumbled thoughts with another diary? If I could add pages to you, I would. For all these years you faithfully have held my words, and you've invited me to come back anytime and read them. You'll never know how much you've helped me become who I am today. You're a mirror. A treasure chest. A gentle reminder of good times and bad. And just as Uncle Bob said when he gave you to me so many years ago, you became a real friend.

Dearest Silent Friend, thank you for giving your empty self to me and allowing me to fill your pages. You know I'll keep you always. I'll visit you many times before my life is over. You'll make me laugh aloud. You'll catch a few more of my salty tears—when I read the words you've been holding for me and when I remember the hurts.

Perhaps one day you'll see an unfamiliar pair of eyes scanning your pages, and you'll feel a different pair of hands holding you. That probably will be my daughter. If,

Lord willing, I marry and have a daughter. I will invite her to read the words you've held so patiently for me because I'll want her to know that what she's feeling is normal. And I'll want her to know that her mother was a goof sometimes. And overly emotional. But more than anything, that her mother was a God-lover.

So please know, my Dear Silent Friend, that this isn't really good-bye. The truth is, you will forever be tucked away in the secret place in my heart.

*From the Secret Place in My Heart: Christy Miller's Diary*
Copyright © 1999
Robin Jones Gunn

Cover by Lookout Design Group, Inc.

Unless otherwise identified, Scripture quotations are from the HOLY BIBLE, NEW INTERNATIONAL VERSION®. Copyright © 1973, 1978, 1984 by International Bible Society. Used by permission of Zondervan Publishing House. All rights reserved. The "NIV" and "New International Version" trademarks are registered in the United States Patent and Trademark Office by International Bible Society. Use of either trademark requires the permission of International Bible Society.

The verse on page 65 is from the Revised Standard Version of the Bible. Copyright 1946, 1952, 1971 by the Division of Christian Education of the National Council of Churches of Christ in the USA. Used by permission.

All rights reserved. No part of this publication may be reproduced, stored in a retrieval system, or transmitted in any form or by any means—electronic, mechanical, photocopying, recording, or otherwise—without the prior written permission of the publisher and copyright owners.

Published by Bethany House Publishers
A Ministry of Bethany Fellowship International
11400 Hampshire Avenue South
Minneapolis, Minnesota 55438
www.bethanyhouse.com

Printed in the United States of America by
Bethany Press International, Minneapolis, Minnesota 55438

**Library of Congress Cataloging-in-Publication Data**

Gunn, Robin Jones, 1955–
    From the secret place in my heart ; Christy Miller's diary / by Robin Jones Gunn.
      p. cm.
    SUMMARY: Fifteen-year-old Christy, who has given her life to God, keeps a diary account of her move to California, experiences at school in Switzerland, and relationship with Todd.
    ISBN 0–7642–2261–9 (pbk.)
    [1. Interpersonal relations Fiction.  2. Christian life Fiction.
3. Diaries Fiction.]  I. Title.
    PZ7.G972  Fr  1999
    [Fic] — dc21
                                         99–6736
                                           CIP

# You Won't Want to Miss

*Until Tomorrow*

**Book One**

in

**Christy and Todd:**
**The College Years!**

**Available June 2000**

# From Robin Jones Gunn

## THE CHRISTY MILLER SERIES

1 • *Summer Promise*
2 • *A Whisper and a Wish*
3 • *Yours Forever*
4 • *Surprise Endings*
5 • *Island Dreamer*
6 • *A Heart Full of Hope*
7 • *True Friends*
8 • *Starry Night*
9 • *Seventeen Wishes*
10 • *A Time to Cherish*
11 • *Sweet Dreams*
12 • *A Promise Is Forever*

*From the Secret Place in My Heart: Christy Miller's Diary*

## THE SIERRA JENSEN SERIES

1 • *Only You, Sierra*
2 • *In Your Dreams*
3 • *Don't You Wish*
4 • *Close Your Eyes*
5 • *Without A Doubt*
6 • *With This Ring*
7 • *Open Your Heart*
8 • *Time Will Tell*
9 • *Now Picture This*
10 • *Hold On Tight*
11 • *Closer Than Ever*
12 • *Take My Hand*

# From Robin Jones Gunn and Wendy Lee Nentwig

*Departures*

# Young Adult Fiction Series From Bethany House Publishers

(Ages 12 and up)

⸺⸺

**CEDAR RIVER DAYDREAMS** • by Judy Baer
Experience the challenges and excitement of high school life with Lexi Leighton and her friends.

**GOLDEN FILLY SERIES** • by Lauraine Snelling
Tricia Evanston races to become the first female jockey to win the sought-after Triple Crown.

**JENNIE MCGRADY MYSTERIES** • by Patricia Rushford
A contemporary Nancy Drew, Jennie McGrady's sleuthing talents bring back readers again and again.

**LIVE! FROM BRENTWOOD HIGH** • by Judy Baer
The staff of an action-packed teen-run news show explores the love, laughter, and tears of high school life.

**PASSPORT TO DANGER** • by Mary Reeves Bell
Constantine Rea, an American living in modern-day Austria, confronts the lasting horrors of the Holocaust.

**THE SPECTRUM CHRONICLES** • by Thomas Locke
Adventure awaits readers in this fantasy series set in another place and time.

**SPRINGSONG BOOKS** • by various authors
Compelling love stories and contemporary themes promise to capture the hearts of readers.

**UNMISTAKABLY COOPER ELLIS** • by Wendy Lee Nentwig
Laugh and cry with Cooper as she strives to balance modeling, faith, and life at her Manhattan high school.

**WHITE DOVE ROMANCES** • by Yvonne Lehman
Romance, suspense, and fast-paced action for teens committed to finding pure love.